Senior Prom

Patricia Aks

SCHOLASTIC INC.
New York Toronto London Auckland Sydney

To Ivy, with love

ISBN 0-590-33553-7

12 11 10 9 8 7 6 5 4 3   6 7 8 9/8 0/9

Printed in the U.S.A.   06

Senior Prom

A Wildfire® Book

WILDFIRE TITLES FROM SCHOLASTIC

I'm Christy by Maud Johnson
Beautiful Girl by Elisabeth Ogilvie
Dreams Can Come True by Jane Claypool Miner
An April Love Story by Caroline B. Cooney
Yours Truly, Love Janie by Ann Reit
Take Care of My Girl by Carol Stanley
Nancy & Nick by Caroline B. Cooney
Senior Class by Jane Claypool Miner
Junior Prom by Patricia Aks
He Loves Me Not by Caroline B. Cooney
Good-bye, Pretty One by Lucille S. Warner
Christy's Choice by Maud Johnson
The Wrong Boy by Carol Stanley
The Boy for Me by Jane Claypool Miner
Phone Calls by Ann Reit
Just You and Me by Ann Martin
Holly in Love by Caroline B. Cooney
Spring Love by Jennifer Sarasin
No Boys? by McClure Jones
That Other Girl by Conrad Nowels
Little Lies by Audrey Johnson
Broken Dreams by Susan Mendonca
Love Games by Deborah Aydt
Miss Perfect by Jill Ross Klevin
On Your Toes by Terry Morris
Christy's Love by Maud Johnson
Nice Girls Don't by Caroline B. Cooney
Christy's Senior Year by Maud Johnson
Kiss and Tell by Helen Cavanagh
The Boy Next Door by Vicky Martin
Angel by Helen Cavanagh
Out of Bounds by Eilen Hehl
Senior Dreams Can Come True by Jane Claypool Miner
Loving That O'Connor Boy by Diane Hoh
Love Signs by M. L. Kennedy
My Summer Love by Elisabeth Ogilvie
Once Upon a Kiss by Susan Mendonca
Kisses for Sale by Judith Enderle
Crazy Crush by Stephanie Gordon Tessler
The Boy Barrier by Jesse DuKore
The Yes Girl by Kathryn Makris
Love to the Rescue by Deborah Kent
Senior Prom by Patricia Aks

One

It's strange how one thing — a person or an event — can change your whole life. That fact came home to me with unexpected force when Ms. Cogswell, our new eleventh-grade English teacher at Teaneck High, asked us to write a paper on the subject.

"You can write on how your attitude changed, or your self-image, or your feelings about someone, because of a particular experience," she elaborated.

There were quite a few groans when she gave us the assignment — not everyone is into writing the way I am, and it's no myth that new teachers are always being tested — but Ms. Cogswell didn't rise to the bait. She's on the young side, prematurely gray, skinny, intense, and passionate about books. She also has a sense of humor.

Instead of bristling at the rather negative reaction, she smiled and said, "I'm not asking you to write an epic, just a couple of pages on something that's made you feel or see life differently. And of course the papers will be confidential."

"Like what?" Fred Campbell asked from the back of the room. Fred is bright, a super athlete, but lackadaisical when it comes to studying. He's only interested in sports, and is so assured of getting a football scholarship to college that he does a minimum of work.

"It can be as dramatic as discovering that half a cup of red wine turns an ordinary stew into a gourmet dish. As a result you might be turned on to cooking forever!"

Even the groaners had to chuckle at that example, and what seemed like a heavy writing assignment suddenly became much more fun. Personally, I couldn't wait to get started.

On the way home Mary Jane Gibson, better known as M. J., my best friend, asked me if I thought it was stupid if she wrote about how losing weight over the summer made her feel like a different person. M. J. is five-foot-two; has black curly hair, sparkling dark eyes, and a bubbly personality. She is definitely cute, but she has always worried about her weight. This past summer she actually shed five pounds.

"Why not?" I told her. "It means a lot to you and your self-image. That's what it's all about."

"It's not exactly earth-shaking that I don't feel like a blimp anymore."

"You never looked like a blimp, M. J."

"You're just being kind. If I were three inches taller, like you, Amy Ross, and weighed in at one hundred and five, I wouldn't complain. Anyhow, I'm five pounds lighter, and I feel like a sylph."

"Or a walking poem," I suggested, and we both giggled.

"What are you writing on?" she asked.

"The Junior Prom," I answered.

"Last spring's Junior Prom?" She looked puzzled.

"That was a turning point in my life."

"I thought it was just a great bash," M. J. said.

"It was more than that to me. Remember how uptight I was about getting invited?" I asked her.

"Well, yes, I do remember that."

"And then how excited I was when Jeff asked me to go with him? It was only a few days before, and I hadn't received one bid, and I was prepared to break a leg or fake pneumonia in order to explain why I wasn't going." My blood still ran cold when I thought how humiliated I would have been.

"It all comes back to me, but how did the Junior Prom change your life?"

"Because . . . because. It's so complicated, but I'll let you see my paper, I promise." We had arrived at my house, and since this was one of the three nights during the week that my mother worked in the administration department of the local hospital, I had to get dinner ready and didn't have time to talk.

"I can't wait. Sounds a lot more interesting than the effect of my summer diet."

"Not necessarily. That's what's important to you, and nobody should knock it."

M. J. grinned. "I don't know what I'd do without you for a support system, Amy."

"And I don't know what I'd do without you."

I waved good-bye, and then let myself into the split-level house that we've lived in since I was a toddler. The house was quiet, which meant my carrot-topped, freckle-faced brother, Kenny, wasn't home yet. I can tell the minute I walk into the house whether he's there or not, because he always leaves a trail from the hall to his room.

Kenny can be a pest, but it's hard for me to stay mad at him long because he is my number one fan. He's discovered girls this year, and calls me his "advisor on women." I try to make him understand that girls have the same feelings as boys. If he bears that in mind and acts natural, he'll do fine. Something I learned the hard way.

I dumped my books in my room, which is the smallest in the house and wouldn't win any prizes in decorating, but I love it. It's furnished like a sitting room, with a hi-rise so I can have a friend for a sleepover. My most prized possession, an electric typewriter that my parents gave me for my birthday last year, sits on my desk. And I have my own bathroom, which means I don't have to share with my brothers.

My brother Greg is two years older than me, and is a freshman at Bowdoin College in Maine. I couldn't believe how much I missed him after only two weeks, even though he spends most of his waking hours teasing me. The truth is, I really love my family. This theory about suffering because you're the middle child is crazy. As Greg puts it, he and Kenny are the staff of life, meaning the bread, and I'm the peanut butter. I wouldn't trade places with anyone!

I went into the kitchen and read the note my mother always leaves for me the days she works.

Amy — meat loaf is in fridge ready to go. Pre-heat oven to 350° and cook for one hour. Everything else can wait till I get home at six. Love, Mom

I had just turned on the oven when I heard the front door opening, followed by a loud thump and a whirring sound. That had to be Kenny making his entrance. Within seconds he appeared in the kitchen, flashed his chipmunk smile, and exclaimed, "Heidi said she was going to the game Saturday, and I said so was I, and she said why don't we go together. I mean all this time I was trying to get my nerve up to ask her and then she turns around and asks me. It's all because I took your advice and acted natural — you know, my usual irresistible self. How can I ever repay you, Aim?"

"For starters, you could try saying hello, and then how about setting the table?"

"Hello, Amy," he said with painstaking deliberation. "Of course I'll set the table, but first I must wash up." Then, as though he had exhausted his reservoir of politeness, he spun out of the room. As usual, he left me shaking my head in despair and smiling at the same time.

I put the meat loaf in the oven, turned on the timer, and went into my room with the idea of doing my homework. I have this theory that if I get most of it done before dinner, I have time afterwards to rap on the phone with my friends, watch tv, or continue my ongoing Scrabble contest with my father. My mother says she doesn't want to compete with the "wordsmiths" in the family, and she likes to work on the scatter rug she's been finishing for the past two years.

I like to save the best till last. Therefore I planned to do my math first, next memorize irregular verbs for French, read two chapters in American history, and then do my paper for English. I attacked my geometry, and was working on the second problem when I started thinking about Ms. Cogswell's assignment. There was no point in fighting it; my head was too crowded with thoughts about how the Junior Prom had changed my life for me to concentrate on anything else. Might as well do my paper, so I could work on my other homework.

I plunked away at my typewriter nonstop

for almost an hour and could have gone on much longer if Kenny hadn't banged on my door and shouted, "Help! The bell went off!"

It took me a few seconds to figure out what he was carrying on about. "Huh?" I mumbled.

"The bell . . . in the oven. What should I do?"

"Turn it off, Kenny," I said as calmly as possible. Kenny is in seventh grade and not quite as rambunctious as a year ago, but he has occasional lapses.

"The bell or the oven?" he asked impishly, poking his head through the door.

"Both," I replied patiently.

"If it weren't for me, our whole supper would probably go up in smoke and we'd starve the rest of. . . ." His voice faded as he raced down the hall.

"You're right, you're right," I called after him, and turned back to my paper.

It was already too long, but I had to add a final paragraph. Then I read it over, and was astounded at how one event could have had such an impact on my life. All the things Ms. Cogswell had mentioned — attitude, self-image, feelings about someone — had been dramatically affected by the Junior Prom. I was so anxious to be invited that I practically killed myself to be agreeable and change my interests to suit whoever asked me out. I figured if I totally pleased each boy, one of them would invite me to the party-of-the-year. I became an instant expert in basketball, rock music, and gerbils just to please my dates, but instead of impressing them, they were totally turned off. It wasn't until I was myself and behaved naturally that I was "discovered," by Jeff, the only boy I ever really liked anyway.

Jeff was a junior then and worked in the library. I didn't think he knew I was alive, but just when I'd given up all hope of going to the prom, we found each other. We had so much in common! We both loved books and could talk about them endlessly. Neither of us had ever been romantically involved with anyone. And Greg said we even *looked* alike. I wasn't sure if he was teasing me or not, but I was kind of flattered. Not that Jeff could be mistaken for Tom Selleck's brother, but I think he's really cute — average height, skinnyish, permanently tousled dark hair, expressive brown eyes that are magnified by wire-framed glasses and reflect every mood.

I guess I knew I was okay-looking. My father, who does incline to spoil me, has been telling me I'm pretty for as long as I can remember, but only Jeff made me believe it. Jeff gave me confidence in myself that I might never have had — not just about my looks, but about everything. I suppose what it comes down to is that we fell in love at that spring dance. No wonder I believed that the Junior Prom had changed my life!

Two

It was Friday afternoon, the end of September, and I was sitting in a booth at Rico's with M. J. where we awaited the arrival of our two other closest friends, Gail and Terry. We were sipping our Tabs that we'd already bought and paid for at the self-service fountain. Meeting at Rico's every Friday, when school lets out early and no extracurricular activities are planned, had become a tradition for us. It began in tenth grade, and we all assume it will continue through our senior year. We promised one another that no matter what happens the rest of our lives — college, career, marriage, children — we will plan a reunion annually at Rico's.

Early on we made an agreement that if any one of us wanted to be elsewhere — which was a subtle way of saying having a special date with a boy during this precious time — no explanations were necessary.

Strangely enough, that was never a problem. M. J.'s boyfriend, Bud, who she's been going with for more than a year, was never available because he helps out his father in his pharmacy every Friday after school; Gail, who is tall, high-cheekboned, and in keeping with her dramatic style wears her long tawny hair in a single braid, claims these rap sessions are a form of therapy, only much more fun; and Terry, a willowy blonde who is very smart but too cool to let everyone know, and whose indifference drives boys crazy, says her friendship with us is more important than any date. Besides, she explained, there was always Friday and Saturday nights, as well as Sunday afternoon, in which to go out with boys. I, too, believed that this was a special time that I wanted to spend with my girl friends, although Jeff didn't quite see it my way. In fact, when I first mentioned it to him at the beginning of school, he gave me an argument about how he wanted to spend his free time with me.

"But Jeff, these are my best friends! I see them in class, but that doesn't mean we get a chance to talk."

"What about me? I thought you'd rather be with me than anyone."

"I would rather be with you than any boy, but you can't expect me not to see my girl friends. There's no other boy in my life."

It was the first tiff we had — I guess you might call it a lovers' quarrel — and I was both upset and flattered. The conversation took place during our nightly phone call, so I couldn't see his face, but I could imagine him glowering. We'd gotten into the routine of talking to each other at the end of the day, just before I got ready for bed. One of the few rules my parents were strict about was not making or receiving any calls after ten o'clock.

"There better not be a boy," he said with surprising sharpness, and I sensed that he was jealous about something that didn't exist.

"These are my *girl* friends, Jeff, so you have nothing to worry about," I assured him. "I don't expect you not to play in your chess club every Thursday, and that's coed."

That was a really dumb argument, because I work on the paper, *Swen* — news spelled backward — on Thursdays, but he didn't remind me of that. There was a long pause, and finally Jeff said, "I guess you're right, Amy. It's just that . . . that I love you."

"And I love you, too," I said, which was the way we ended all our nightly phone calls.

As I sat there with M. J., my feelings about our "Fridays" were reinforced. I wasn't convinced that Jeff really understood, and I wondered if boys were capable of having the kind of relationship the four of us had. That was exactly the kind of subject we might get into and I thought I would bring it up when M. J. said, "Your paper for English was really great."

I had shown it to her in our last class, American history, while Mr. Wilson, our shaggy-haired, permanently distracted teacher, was expounding on the fine points of the Constitution. Mr. Wilson is a scholar who has had articles published on the Civil War and frequently gets carried away. M. J. and I sit in the back of the room and exchange notes whenever he goes off on one of his tangents. It was a perfect time for M. J. to read my paper.

"Thanks," I said. "It could have been twice as long, but I didn't want to put Ms. Cogswell to sleep."

"Not possible! You were talking about life and changes."

"I guess we've all changed a lot since last year."

"You most of all, Amy." That was Gail's voice and I was momentarily taken aback because I hadn't noticed Gail and Terry come in. They slid into the booth beside us.

"That's true," Terry said.

"For the better of course," I said coyly.

"Of course," Gail said. "You're much more relaxed."

"That's what love will do," Terry stated. "I wish I had a boyfriend I could count on like you have Jeff, and M. J. has Bud."

"Thought you liked playing the field," M. J. said.

"It's fun, but I think I'm ready to settle down." Terry sounded wistful.

"You sound like you want to get married," Gail teased.

"Not quite," Terry said, "but I've been juggling too many boys for too long."

"Fighting them off, is more like it," M. J. remarked.

"My problem is, I get these mad crushes, and then as soon as they're reciprocated, I lose interest," Gail admitted. "It's like a game, but I wouldn't mind a serious romance now, either."

"It'll happen to you like it did to me probably," I said. "When you least expect it. At least you've had a series of boyfriends — a phase that passed me by completely. I mean I never had boys vying for my attention the way you all do . . . or did."

"I never thought of that," M. J. said. "I actually did have three miniromances before Bud and I started going together. He did, too, so we both are very experienced." She couldn't help laughing at herself after this pronouncement.

"Just the opposite with me and Jeff. Neither of us was ever interested in a member of the opposite sex before. I guess from that point of view, we're very *in*experienced."

"But you both read a lot," Gail joked, and then we all cracked up.

"Actually, we never run out of conversation because we always can talk about books." I was being serious.

"Would you say that's what brought you together?" Gail asked.

"That's part of it. The main reason,

though, is that we really were attracted to each other." I sighed dreamily.

"You are lucky," Gail commented.

"I know," I said. "And there are so many fringe benefits."

"Like what?"

"Besides really liking each other, the best part of having a guy is that I don't have to worry about who'll take me to the Senior Prom!"

"And that's why you're so relaxed," Terry said, smiling.

I knew she was kidding me, but there was a lot of truth in that statement. After the Junior Prom, my anxiety about having a date for any special event disappeared. Like it was the most natural thing in the world that we would go to the Kick-off Dance after the first football game. And I didn't have to worry about having a partner for the square dances, or the Christmas parties, or anything. There was no longer a question of whether I'd be asked, but rather what time Jeff should pick me up.

All summer we'd gotten into a pattern of spending our free time together. I had a job as a "go-fer" on the *Teaneck Gazette*, a small weekly newspaper that provided all the local news and advertising. It didn't bother me at all that my tasks included filing letters and sharpening pencils, and that I made very little money. I just loved being around an honest-to-goodness newspaper. And Jeff worked at the local bookstore, replacing the permanent staff when they went on vacation. We both lived for the weekends when we could spend long stretches of time together. It was hard for me to remember a time when we hadn't been going together.

"Yes, I certainly am more relaxed," I admitted.

"Have you had your first fight?" Gail asked. She was not famous for her subtlety.

"Sort of," I answered. "As a matter of fact, it was about the four of us."

"About us?" Gail raised her voice several octaves. "Why us?"

"Well, Jeff didn't exactly appreciate me not spending Friday afternoons with him."

"Uh-oh," Terry said ominously. "Sounds like the green-eyed monster is hovering over him."

"But you're here," M. J. observed, "so it couldn't have been too serious."

"No, it wasn't, but I wonder if boys can ever understand friendship the way we do."

"Don't think so," Terry said thoughtfully.

"I think boys always have to be *doing* something together — working on a project, or playing a game, or competing," M. J. offered.

"They don't know what they're missing," Gail said. "I personally wouldn't give up these Fridays for anything!"

"Me neither," M. J. said.

And the four of us all nodded our heads in agreement.

Three

My parents knew that Jeff was my first real boyfriend. That fact was an endless source of teasing for Greg and Kenny, but my mother and father were too diplomatic to make fun of something I took so seriously. Also, for quite a while, they never had more than a three-minute conversation with Jeff, and that took place only when he came to the house to pick me up. I wasn't exactly avoiding their getting to know him, but somewhere I was worried about whether or not they'd hit it off.

Then, after the summer, my mother suggested that Jeff have brunch with us one Sunday. I wanted to invite him, but I was a little nervous about how it would go. This was one of the times I wished Greg had been around. He was great at getting me through awkward situations. I woke up that Sunday morning missing him more than ever.

Jeff's on the shy side, and not the type to take over the conversation. What if there were long silences, where no one could think of anything to say? I knew I was being ridiculous, because my parents always made my friends feel welcome. I guess Jeff meant so much to me that I didn't want anything to come between us. So far nothing had. This was like a final obstacle that had to be overcome. In an imaginary conversation with Greg, I could hear him saying, "But dummy, it's not an obstacle. They'll probably get along great."

To be on the safe side, I told my parents we planned to go to Terry's house at two o'clock. She'd invited some kids over to watch a Charlie Chaplin movie on video. Personally, I wasn't that anxious to see it, but I wanted an excuse to split if the brunch turned into a disaster.

Jeff arrived promptly at noon, and after an exchange of hellos and handshakes, my mother herded us into our eat-in kitchen and gave each of us an assignment. She prepared the French toast, Jeff and I had the bacon detail, Kenny set the table, and my father brewed the coffee. I realized that my mother's technique in making Jeff feel right at home was not to treat him as a guest.

When my father learned that Jeff was a senior editor on the school literary magazine, the *Scroll*, and wanted to have a career in publishing, the conversation took off. Then Jeff pointed out that my job as feature editor for the *Swen* was remarkable for a junior. Kenny provided comic relief by describing his dilemma of having accepted the invitations of two girls to the opening football game because he didn't want to disappoint either of them. By the time we'd polished off brunch and cleaned up, it was almost two o'clock and my mother had to remind me about going to Terry's.

"Oh yeah," I said. "I guess we should leave." I couldn't believe how the time had flown.

"I hope you'll join us soon again, Jeff," my mother said.

"I'd love to, Mrs. Ross. Any time Amy gives me the word."

"And next time come early so you can teach me how to play chess. Amy says you're really good," Kenny piped up.

"Does she always talk behind my back?"

"Always, always, always."

"With that kind of reputation, how can I say no to you, Kenny?"

"You can't." Kenny was so serious that we burst out laughing.

We were still smiling as we left the house and headed for Terry's. Jeff took my hand in his.

"I have to confess, Amy, I was worried about today. But your family is really great."

"I was worried, too," I admitted, "but everything went perfectly."

"Couldn't have been better."

"That's what I think." I squeezed his hand

and breathed deeply. At that moment, I honestly believed I was the luckiest girl in the world.

We could hear a din of voices and disco music as we waited for someone to answer the doorbell at Terry's house.

"Thought you said this was going to be a quiet afternoon," Jeff said.

"I thought so," I said, and we both shrugged our shoulders just as Terry opened the door.

Seeing our surprised look, she quickly explained. "This thing has mushroomed since I last spoke to you, Amy. What started out as a few kids coming over to watch a flick, has developed into a major party. Len wanted to come over and play a new piece he's written for the band, featuring his guitar, naturally. Then Alex and Jerry called, and since I didn't want the boys to outnumber us, I invited some more girls over. Most of the kids are in the family room, discoing."

"What about the movie?" Jeff asked.

"That's about to begin in the den. You can watch the flick or dance, or do both."

"I'm for the movie," Jeff said.

"We'll start out there," I agreed.

"My folks are making a batch of spaghetti, so if you get hungry, you know where to go."

"Thanks, Terry," I said, and Jeff and I headed for the den where a few kids were draped around the room.

Alex, who is short, pudgy, and a stand-up

comedian, had obviously taken over the showing of the film. He waved to us as everyone said hello, and then said, "Take your seats, please," which meant us. We settled down in the back of the room, me on a hassock and Jeff on the floor, and Alex continued.

"There will be one fifteen-minute intermission where you can freshen up, find refreshments, or leave. Silence, please. Camera! Action! Shoot!"

Everyone in that room, except me, was a Charlie Chaplin fan, and chuckled nonstop at his antics. I was the only one who wasn't totally absorbed, but it was nice to be sitting in a dark room, my hand resting on Jeff's shoulder. However, after about forty minutes I was glad that Alex turned off the video tape, flicked on the lights, and told us the show would resume in exactly fifteen minutes.

Jeff said he was going to "freshen up," and I drifted into the family room where half a dozen couples were gyrating to the music.

Jerry, the editor of the *Swen*, was across the room, watching the dancers and keeping time to the music with his body. He saw me come in, and danced over to where I was standing. Jerry is a senior, sharp-faced, lanky, and an outstanding track star as well as a superb editor. He's popular with everyone, and a lot of fun, but he can be serious, too. Although I'm not too great at accepting criticism of my writing or my editorial judgment, he's always very kind with his suggestions — not at all like last year's editor, Bob Gilman, who had the sensitivity of an overheated gorilla. If Bob was wildly enthusiastic about an article, he'd nod his head and mumble, "Not bad." Jerry, on the other hand, had gone so far as to tell me I had a major talent.

Jerry and I rarely talked about anything but the *Swen*, but it was too noisy to have a normal conversation. Without even asking, or missing a beat, he pulled me into the center of the room. Jerry's grace as an athlete was evident in his dancing, and he twirled me around with such agility that I was soon caught up in the vibrant mood of the dancers.

It took all my concentration to keep up with Jerry's maneuvers, and I lost complete track of time. Therefore it came as a surprise to see Jeff standing at the edge of the crowd, motioning me toward him. It flashed through my mind that the intermission was over and the movie was about to continue, but I much preferred dancing. Jerry had executed a step where we briefly ended up back-to-back, which gave me the opportunity to wave to Jeff, point to my feet, and shout, "Let's dance!" At that moment, Jerry circled around me, blocking my view, and I couldn't see Jeff's reaction. But once Jerry was no longer in front of me, and I looked for Jeff, he was gone.

Before I had time to think, Jerry grabbed me by the waist and swung me around so that my feet were literally off the ground. Fortunately, I was dressed for the occasion in a new baggy-jeans outfit, which made me feel free to indulge in these acrobatics. I was so pleased with myself for being able to keep up with Jerry, that I didn't give a thought to Charlie Chaplin. And we danced — if you can call it that — until we both were gasping for breath.

"You're really good," Jerry said, guiding me off the floor.

"I love to dance, and you're terrific," I said.

"Maybe we should take our act on the road."

"Not a bad idea, but right now I think I better find Jeff."

"As soon as I find someone who's light enough to lift, she's off and running into the arms of another man." Jerry smiled and blew me a kiss as I moved away, and I saw him heading toward a group of girls who were beckoning him from a pile of floor pillows at the far side of the room.

It took me a few minutes to adjust my eyes to the dimly lit den. Then I saw Jeff sitting by himself on a loveseat against the wall. As unobtrusively as possible I made my way toward him. He didn't acknowledge my presence as I sank down beside him, and I assumed he was totally absorbed in the film. I tried to get into it, too, but I'd missed so much that the story didn't make sense, and I waited patiently for it to end. Meanwhile, I rubbed the back of my hand against Jeff's, hoping he would hold mine. But he didn't take the hint and I inched away, giving up my attempt to have any physical contact. I could see from the digital clock on the tv that I'd only been sitting there ten minutes, but the vibes I was getting from Jeff made it seem much longer.

Another ten minutes and it was over. Alex flicked on the lights, muttered something about Chaplin being a genius, and everyone straggled out of the room, leaving me and Jeff alone.

"You're looking pretty glum, considering this is a comedy," I remarked.

"Me, glum? Whatever makes you say that?"

"Well, for one thing, the corners of your mouth are turned down, a sure sign that you're not smiling."

"You're very observant." Jeff's voice was steely.

"What's wrong?" I asked.

"You really don't know?"

"All I know is that I preferred dancing to watching a movie. Is that what's bugging you?"

"You guessed it."

"But why are you mad?"

"Because we started out watching a movie together, and the next thing I know you've disappeared and don't even bother to tell me where you're going."

"I didn't exactly leave the country! I might have been out of your sight all of seven minutes! You found me in the next room, and

I even pointed to my feet and said, 'Let's dance.' The next thing I knew, you had disappeared."

"I thought we were going together, Amy."

"We are."

"But that obviously means something different to each of us."

"Does it mean that I can't even dance with somebody else?"

"You didn't see me asking some other girl to dance, did you?"

"I wouldn't have cared if you did."

"You wouldn't?" Jeff seemed baffled by my answer.

"Of course not. In fact, why don't you try it right now and see what happens. I don't think either of us will vanish into smoke."

Jeff looked at me lovingly and almost managed to smile. "Maybe I just love you too much."

"Not possible, Jeff!" I kissed him impulsively on the cheek and started to get up.

"Not so fast," Jeff said, and pulled me down.

Then he wrapped his arms around me, and slowly pressed his lips against mine. We might have stayed in that embrace all afternoon if a loud voice hadn't disturbed us. It was Alex, in his usual obstreperous manner, saying, "You guys can do that later. Right now, Len is playing his new number, and he wants everyone to hear it."

"We'll be right there," I said, as Alex disappeared, probably to round up some other strays.

"One more kiss," Jeff insisted, as I started to get up again, "so that I know you love me."

I fell back into his arms, and kissed him again on the mouth.

"You do love me," he whispered in my ear.

I wasn't sure if that was a question or a statement, but I wasn't taking any chances. "You know it!" I said, and sighed happily. Our "misunderstanding" seemed never to have happened.

Four

I loved my job on the *Swen* as feature editor, but since the position had always been filled by a senior, I worked extra hard to prove I was worthy. Not only did I edit other people's stories, but I wrote some myself. The writing assignments were made by Jerry and the managing editor, Carl, a wiry, nonstop talker whose energy was contagious. The entire staff agreed that, if necessary, Carl could put out an issue single-handed. He was also an excellent cartoonist, whose comic presentations were one of the *Swen*'s most popular features.

Ms. Newman was our faculty advisor, and quietly got across her strong opinions with a minimum of fuss. She was my tenth-grade English teacher, and I have to admit I was her pet. At the end of last year she told me that I was one of the most promising writers she'd come across in seven years of teaching.

It was the biggest compliment of my life. I knew it was because of her recommendation that I was given some of the plum stories to write.

In each issue, there is an interview with an outstanding student, such as the head of the student council, the leader of a rock group, or a star athlete. These interviews are usually routine and done well in advance. The one scheduled for the November 8 issue was with a graffiti artist who signed his work "Camel." Camel was president of the art club and was making a reputation — not necessarily favorable — throughout the community. His interview had been wrapped up a week early.

Two days before the issue was to close, Jerry called an emergency meeting of the *Swen*. We gathered in the office as soon as classes were over. The office was an old study hall converted into a newsroom, and had several typewriters; a long table, designated the conference table; and a bunch of desks that were assigned to each editor. The staff settled down at the conference table, and Jerry didn't waste any time telling us why we were there.

"We're pulling the interview with Camel, and doing one with Mark Thompson."

Mark was captain of the football team, and not only highly intelligent, but an outstanding quarterback.

"Why?" asked Sherry, the intense, precise

copy editor. Sherry questioned everything, even when she knew the answers.

"Because of the controversy raging over Billy Simpson," Jerry explained.

Billy was unquestionably the most versatile player on the team. He was known as the Streak because of his incredible speed, and his teammates, his opponents, and every spectator knew he was responsible for Teaneck's undefeated season.

The problem was that Billy wasn't too interested in the academic side of school. He'd always managed to squeak by, until he came across Mr. Lacey. Lacey taught trigonometry and believed that math had an "elegance" vastly superior to any maneuver executed on the football field. He did not approve of Billy's average in his classroom, which hovered around a D minus, and he spearheaded a drive to bench athletes who got less than passing grades.

The news that Billy might be benched spread quickly. The last game of the season, against Teaneck's arch rival, Essex Fells, was scheduled Thanksgiving weekend. Our undefeated team would go into a tailspin, physically as well as psychologically, if Billy didn't play. That was all anyone could talk about, and the *Swen* was deluged with letters to the editor arguing both sides. Not surprisingly, some of the nonathletic "brains" were on Lacey's side, but the majority came out for Billy. Through all this, Mark kept a very low profile, but everyone was curious about his point of view.

"The controversy over Lacey's edict is the most important news of the week — possibly the year — and maybe of the century. In fact, the decision made regarding Billy may affect every member of the student body, and certainly every athlete who crosses Teaneck's threshold, for generations to come." I'd never seen Jerry so serious.

"What are we supposed to do?" Sherry asked.

"We've already given the story plenty of exposure, but the one person everyone would like to hear from is Mark . . . and as soon as possible."

"Like today," Carl added. "Someone has to reach him when he finishes practice." He glanced at his watch. "In about forty minutes, to be exact."

"Who can do it?" Jerry looked around the room, but no one volunteered, and his gaze finally settled on me.

"I . . . I can," I stammered. It flashed through my mind that this was the day my mother worked at the hospital, and I was supposed to get dinner ready. But I figured I could call home and get Kenny to take over for me. He'd be so excited that I was interviewing Mark, he'd do anything for me.

"If Amy can buttonhole him when he gets off the field and write it up tonight, I'll edit it . . . over the phone, if necessary."

"And I can copyedit it during my study period, which happens to be my second class in the morning . . . a stupid time for a study period, but — "

"That's great, Sherry," Jerry interrupted her.

Then Carl turned to Maggie, the photography editor. "Do you have any head shots?"

"A few. It's just a matter of choice."

"Then we're all set. And thank you for coming," Jerry said. "I should have thought of this earlier, but it didn't occur to me until the middle of the night that what Mark has to say could affect the administration's decision."

Jerry stood up, indicating the meeting was over, and everyone drifted out. I hung back and jotted down some questions that I thought would be suitable to ask. Jerry leaned against the table, watching me.

"I was hoping you'd be the one," he said. "You know, Mark really doesn't like publicity, but I think you can handle him."

"I hope so," I said. "Actually, I think it's a privilege to do the interview with him, and the only reason I hesitated is because I'm supposed to get home right after school tonight. Which reminds me, I better call my brother."

I reached down for my canvas bag and as I started to sit up I felt Jerry's hand on my shoulder. He looked at me intently, gently squeezed my shoulder, and said, almost in a whisper, "Thanks, Amy, for everything."

"Let's hope it works," I said briskly, trying to ignore any double meanings, and fumbled in my bag for a coin.

"Here, the least I can do is pay for your phone call." Jerry handed me a quarter, and smiled.

"Thanks," I said, pushing back my chair. "Now I better get going or I'll blow the whole thing."

I hurried out, without looking back, not sure why I was suddenly breathing so hard, and wondering whether I was running to my assignment or away from Jerry.

Fortunately, Kenny was home and answered the phone immediately. As I expected, he was prepared to do everything, including the dishes.

"An interview with Mark Thompson. Wow! I hope you get a by-line. Then at least everyone will know it's my sister who — "

"Right, Kenny, right. Now I've really got to go, and thanks for taking care of supper."

"No problem. All it is is leftover chicken casserole, and all I have to do is heat it up, and make the salad, and — "

"Later," I said, cutting him short, and hung up.

I made my way out the side door to the athletic grounds, trying to collect my thoughts so I wouldn't come across as a nerd when I started questioning Mark. The team was doing some laps around the field, and I climbed up a few rows of bleachers and watched. After about ten minutes, Coach blew his whistle, and the players trotted off the field. Mark exchanged a few words with Coach, which meant he was the last to head for the gym. That gave me the perfect opportunity to catch him alone.

"Hi," I began, running up to him. "I'm Amy Ross and — "

"I know who you are. I read\ the *Swen* and you're the feature editor."

"That's right." I was so surprised and pleased that for a second I couldn't think of anything to say.

"Did you want to see me?"

"Yes, that's why I'm here. I . . . I wondered if I could ask you some questions."

"What about?"

"About Billy Simpson and Mr. Lacey," I said. "I mean I'm sure you've thought about it." I could have kicked myself then, because this wasn't at all what I'd planned. I was going to ease him into the interview, ask him a lot of routine questions about when he got his first football, and whether he was going out for the team in college. Then I would get to the good stuff.

"You don't mess around, do you, Amy?" He smiled at me indulgently, and I felt like a two-year-old.

"Well, I heard you didn't like a lot of publicity, and the *Swen* wanted to do this interview with you for the issue that's supposed to be at the printer today, and we have to pull the one on Camel in order to make room, and — "

"Look, if you wait for me, I'll take a quick shower and change, and we can talk about this while I walk you home."

"You mean it?" I was flabbergasted. "But I thought you didn't like to talk about yourself." Another idiot remark.

"I don't. But this issue is important, and I've thought a lot about it. Besides, I like your style, Amy."

"I'll wait for you right here," I said, pointing to the bench.

"It won't take me long," he said, and hurried off.

I sat there, thinking how lucky I was that I'd gotten right to the point. If I'd gone with my original plan, he might have put me off. So far everything had gone perfectly — Kenny was home, covering for me; Mark was available and willing; I could pound out the story tonight without any problem.

Before I knew it, Mark had changed into jeans and a pale blue turtleneck, and was loping toward me. He was considered the heartthrob of the senior class, and although I'd never thought much about him before, I could see why. His wavy hair, still damp from the shower, was the color of coal, and his eyes were incredibly blue. He had a small scar on his right cheekbone, which actually added to his otherwise flawless good looks.

No wonder he was Teaneck High's dream-boy.

Strangely enough, I'd never been particularly attracted to handsome boys, and Mark was no exception. I couldn't care less about impressing him. All I wanted was a good interview.

"Where do you live?" he asked.

"On Cranberry Street."

"That's not too far. If we go at a normal pace, you'll know more than you need to fill up space."

"Go slow, because I've got to take notes," I said, getting a pad and pencil out of my bag.

"Don't worry, I want you to get it right."

I could see that Mark was just as serious as I was, and I plunged right in with a key question: "What do you think about Lacey's plan to bench Billy?"

"It'll be a disaster for the team."

"So you're against it."

"I didn't say that. Actually, I think Lacey's got a point. Nobody wants Teaneck to get the reputation of being a school for dumb jocks."

"So you think Billy shouldn't be allowed to play."

"Not if he doesn't improve his grades."

"But Teaneck won't stand a chance against Essex Fells."

"I'm afraid that's true."

"I didn't see Billy at practice today. Has he given up?"

Mark took a deep breath. "Well," he began, "I guess it's okay to talk about it now, because the test is tomorrow."

"What test?"

"Lacey's not quite as tough as he appears. Coach and I and Billy talked to him about ten days ago. He said if Billy got a passing grade on the make-up test, he'll be allowed to play. We're keeping our fingers crossed."

"You think it can happen?"

"I've been helping Billy every day — although that's not for publication — and I'm pretty sure he can do it."

"That's fantastic! And what a scoop!"

"The point is, Billy isn't dumb, he's just plain lazy."

"He's brought the whole issue to a head."

"That's right. He can be a real hero. . . ."

We had arrived at the path leading to my house and I was tingling with excitement. Not only did I have a decent interview with Mark, but a great news story as well.

"Thanks for talking to me," I said.

"Hope you've got everything you need."

"I think so. Only I never got around to asking you when you got your first football."

"Who cares?" he said, and waved good-bye as I hurried into the house.

I couldn't wait until supper was over so I could type up my notes. Kenny bombarded me with questions about Mark, and I promised him he'd be the first one to see the interview once I got it into any sort of shape.

"In that case, I really will do the dishes," he said, and I raced into my room as soon as I finished dessert.

After rewriting the piece three times, I gave it to Kenny to read, and his reaction was exactly what I'd hoped for. First he was surprised that Mark wouldn't be solely in favor of letting Billy play, then he saw the wisdom of maintaining Teaneck's high academic standards, and finally he was just as excited as I was to learn that Billy had been "coached" in trig and would probably meet Lacey's requirements.

Then I called Jerry and read the interview to him over the phone. He said it was a terrific job, and I was floating on air. It took me a while to settle down, but I finally got around to doing my homework. I figured I'd wait until I'd done at least half before calling Jeff and telling him the good news. I'd been working about twenty minutes when Kenny burst into my room.

"I forgot to tell you, Jeff called this afternoon. He said something about bringing over some book that just came into the library. He was surprised you weren't home, but I told him you had to see Mark Thompson."

"I'll call him as soon as I finish memorizing these French idioms. That'll be my reward."

I worked another fifteen minutes, and then I dialed Jeff's number. As soon as he answered and said hello, I knew something was wrong.

"You okay?" I asked.

"Not really," he answered.

"What's the matter?"

"For starters I expected you to be home this afternoon. A new collection of Grace Paley's short stories came into the library and I was going to bring it over. Lucky I bothered to call first."

"I had to see Mark Thompson."

"So I heard."

"It was kind of an emergency, because we had to get this interview in by tomorrow."

"You could have told me."

"I didn't get a chance. Everything happened so fast that the only one I could reach was Kenny. Anyhow, the interview went really well. Jerry said it was terrific!"

"You mean you've already spoken to Jerry about it?" Jeff's voice was like ice.

"I told you it was an emergency. Jerry wanted to edit it over the phone."

"I'm surprised you didn't run over to his house so you could go over it together."

"Jeff, you're being ridiculous! I've told you everything that happened, exactly the way it happened. I'm sorry if I didn't call right away, but Kenny didn't give me the message until just a little while ago. Don't you believe me?"

I could hear Jeff sigh, and then he murmured, "I believe you, Amy. I guess my imagination was working overtime."

"I guess so."

"I can't help being jealous."

"I've noticed." I chuckled a little to take the edge off my sarcasm.

"I'll bring you the book tomorrow." He sounded contrite.

"Thanks," I said.

"I love you, Amy." His voice was normal again.

"Me, too," I said, but for the first time I had trouble getting the words out.

F*ive*

My story on Mark was a big success and everyone complimented me. I should have been euphoric, because Billy did pass the test and I had the inside scoop. But ever since the day of the interview I felt vaguely disturbed about Jeff. No matter how hard I tried, I couldn't forget his unreasonable suspicions. If he didn't trust me, then. . . . I just didn't want to think about it.

It was the Friday after the *Swen* had come out with my interview, and I was sitting with my friends at Rico's.

"What an opportunity you had to be with Mark Thompson — alone!" Gail exclaimed.

"Never thought about it that way." I was being honest.

"You've got to admit, he's the best-looking boy around," Terry remarked.

"Not my type," I said.

"Amy only has eyes for Jeff," M. J. said.

"Guess so," I murmured.

"You guess so?" Gail looked at me in astonishment, but I didn't say anything.

"Sometimes I think having a boyfriend creates as many problems as not having a boyfriend," Gail went on, "but I'd like to try it."

" 'The course of true love never did run smooth.' " Terry quoted Shakespeare.

Everyone chuckled, except me, and M. J. tactfully changed the subject.

"Speaking of true love, I've got to get my parents a twentieth-anniversary present. Any ideas?"

There were a lot of suggestions, and the girls outdid themselves thinking up bizarre presents, including "his" and "her" pet elephants. They thought every idea they had was hilarious, and I pretended I did, too, but I couldn't fool M. J.

On the way home, after we'd left Gail and Terry, M. J. asked, "Is something bothering you?"

"Sort of," I answered. "It's about me and Jeff."

"But you don't want to talk about it."

"Not right now. I'm hoping maybe the problem will go away."

"You mean if you don't face it, it'll disappear?"

"Something like that."

M. J. looked skeptical, but she said, "Maybe you're right."

"I sure hope so. If anything happens between me and Jeff, who will I go with to the Senior Prom?"

M. J. burst out laughing. "You're not serious, Amy?"

"No," I said, smiling weakly, "I'm just trying to keep my sense of humor."

I was kidding about the Senior Prom, but the idea of having a major rift with Jeff was something I didn't want to think about. He must have felt the same way, because neither of us mentioned the tense phone conversation that took place the night of the interview, and for the next few days everything was back to normal. I think we both bent over backwards to be accommodating.

Then one Thursday afternoon, Carl asked me to stay a few minutes after the regular staff meeting in the *Swen* office. He wanted me, Jerry, and Don, the art editor, to go over some cartoons he'd done, and decide which one would be appropriate for the next issue.

I waited at my desk until the rest of the staff had gone, and Carl spread the cartoons out in front of me. Jerry and Don stood behind me so that we could all look at them. Each one had a different theme, and they were all deliciously funny.

"They're all so good, it's hard to choose," Don said.

"I think so, too," Jerry agreed. He had clapped his hand on my shoulder and was bending over so that his chin grazed the top of my head. "Which do you like, Amy?"

"We can't miss with any of them."

"Let's make a decision so I can get it down to scale." Don was getting impatient.

"Let's go with this one." Jerry's hand brushed my arm as he reached for a cartoon called "Trashing the Environment."

"I think that's a good choice, because we have an editorial on the environment, and this will fit right in," I pointed out.

"Let it roll," Carl said, and moved away from my desk.

Just at that moment, we noticed someone standing in the doorway. To my surprise it was Jeff, whose chess club meets on Thursday and ordinarily lasts until the final bell rings. I wasn't sure how long he'd been standing there.

"Hi, Jeff," I greeted him. "I didn't expect to see you."

"I gathered that," he said coldly, and stormed off without another word.

"Oh no," I muttered under my breath, and busily cleaned off my desk. I knew Jerry, Carl, and Don were watching me, and I was really embarrassed. The silence seemed interminable, but finally Carl mumbled something about being pleased that we liked all his cartoons. Then Jerry and Don immediately started talking about having Carl do a comic strip for one issue.

I knew they were trying to cover up for the awkward situation Jeff had created, but I didn't know what to say. I got my things together and headed for the door without looking back.

"See ya," I said, and hurried down the hall.

I thought that maybe Jeff would be waiting for me outside the school, but there was no sign of him. He knew I would be leaving soon, so he must have really rushed off in order to guarantee *not* seeing me.

There was no reason for me to rush, and I walked home slowly, my head whirring with a jumble of feelings. For a while Jeff had kept a lid on his jealousy, and I had rearranged my plans a few times in order not to provoke him. But I guess we were play-acting, and our real needs and desires were bound to surface.

When I got home, the delicious aroma of braised beef in wine sauce floated into the hall. I knew my mother must have been in one of her creative cooking moods, and I went directly into the kitchen.

"Hi, honey," she said. "I'm making your favorite dish."

"I could tell the minute I walked in," I said, and gave her a peck on the cheek.

"Dad got home a few minutes ago, and this should be done soon. We'll sit down in about a half hour."

"Okay. I'll get washed up, and maybe even start my homework."

"Good idea." My mother continued seasoning the gravy, and I started to leave the kitchen.

"Did anyone call?" I asked in an offhand manner.

"No, nobody called," she answered without looking up. "All your friends know you stay late on Thursdays."

"That's true," I said, feeling my heart drop.

I really didn't expect Jeff to cool down so soon, but I was still disappointed that he hadn't telephoned. I was thinking so hard about him that I literally bumped into my father in the hall.

"Heads up, Aim," he said, and gave me a hug.

"Oh, hi, Daddy. I didn't see you."

"You must have had a rough day at school," he teased. "I can practically see the wheels grinding in your head."

"It was okay," I said. Usually my dad and I banter back and forth, but I wasn't in the mood. "Gotta dump my things." I brushed past him and headed for my room.

I pulled my American history book out of my bag, flopped down on my bed, and started to read the assigned chapter. I must have read the first paragraph three times before I gave up. I kept thinking about Jeff and hoping he would call. I thought of the worst — that Jeff had been standing at the door of the *Swen* office the whole time we'd been going over the cartoons, and that he must have misinterpreted the scene.

There I was totally enjoying myself with three boys, all of them leaning over me.

Jerry with his hand on my shoulder, and his head close enough to mine to kiss me. Besides the physical proximity, he wanted my opinion about which cartoon I thought we should use. It was all very innocent from my point of view. . . .

"Amy, are you alive?" That was Kenny, interrupting my thoughts. "We're all waiting for you."

"Oh, okay," I mumbled, "I'll be right there."

I went into my bathroom to wash up and run a comb through my hair, and then hurried into the dining room where my mother was dishing out the veggies and my father was slicing the roast. "Sorry," I said, and slid into my chair.

"Amy just loves doing homework," Kenny said. "She'd rather work than eat."

"Why don't you try that sometime," I said.

"What's bugging you?" Kenny asked. He wasn't used to me not joking with him.

"Forget it," I barked.

The one thing my parents can't stand is to have bickering at mealtime, and normally we manage to oblige. I knew I wasn't able to cope with Kenny's kidding, so I decided to shut up. If I didn't keep a tight rein on my feelings, I might explode or burst into tears.

If my parents thought something was wrong, they had the good sense not to confront me. Instead, my mother told us about how all the records at the hospital where she worked were being computerized and she planned to take a course in word processing.

"Might as well enter the twentieth century," she said, laughing.

"Great idea, dear," my father encouraged her.

"I think so, too," Kenny piped up, "and I can show you how. There's a computer room at school and it's the best course I have. Press a button, and zap! Don't have to think that much."

"We have one at the office, and it has simplified everything. Sometimes I wonder how we managed without it," my father said.

I've noticed that computing is as addictive as chocolate and can be discussed endlessly — at least in my family. I was still too enamored of my electric typewriter to care much about what they were saying. Besides, I was preoccupied with Jeff.

While their voices buzzed around me, I tried to think what Jeff would say when he called. Maybe he'll tell me he was sorry, and then I could be generous and accept his apology with grace. Or maybe he would accuse me of being disloyal and —

"Seconds, Amy?" my mother asked.

"Seconds?" I repeated, not sure what she was talking about.

"Something more to eat." She looked puzzled that I was being so dense.

"Oh, no, thanks," I said.

"What's wrong with you tonight, Amy?" Kenny asked. "You're acting really spacey."

"Do you mind keeping your observations

to yourself?" I was not in the mood for Kenny's cuteness.

"It's a free country, isn't it?" He was not easily put down.

"Hey, you two, cut it out. If you want to do battle, save it until after dessert," my father said.

"Come help me dish out the baked apples, Amy," my mother said. That was her subtle way of getting us both to shut up, and I followed her into the kitchen.

Just at that moment, the phone rang. My heart started pounding as I picked up the receiver that was hung on the wall just inside the kitchen door.

"Is Kenny there?" a girl with a squeaky voice asked.

"Yes, he's here. But we're just about to have dessert."

"Tell him this is Missy, and he should call as soon as he can."

"Okay." I hung up, and tried not to show I was upset. I glanced at the clock, and told myself it was only seven, and there was plenty of time for Jeff to call.

"Who was that?" Kenny asked.

"Missy," I mumbled.

"You might have told me."

"We're not supposed to talk on the phone at mealtime."

"I know that. All I wanted was the message."

"And I gave it to you. What more do you want?"

"Come on, guys," my father said. "We've only got one course to go."

I turned toward my mother and waited while she put a dollop of whipped cream on each baked apple. She handed me one of the desserts and spoke softly, so that no one else could hear. "The hardest thing in the world is not to take it out on everyone else when you have a problem."

"I know, Mom. It's just that I was expecting Jeff to call. Something happened today and . . . I think he may be mad at me."

"You can always call him, you know. Then you'll find out for sure."

I nodded my head, knowing she was right, but afraid of what the consequences would be.

Six

There is a phone in the hall that Kenny, Greg, and I share. It has a long extension cord and I can pull it into my room. This guarantees privacy, and is the next best thing to having my own phone.

That night the phone must have rung six or seven times, and each time I held my breath. Three of the calls were for me — the usual checking in with M. J., Terry, and Gail — but not a word from Jeff. At quarter to ten, I decided to take my mother's advice. I dragged the phone into my room, closed the door, and dialed Jeff's number.

"Hello," I said as normally as possible when he answered. Then I waited for him to say something . . . and waited . . . and waited.

"No point in playing games," I went on. "I wanted to talk to you and I was hoping you'd call."

"Why should I?"

"For starters, I wondered why you didn't wait for me at the *Swen* office, or at least outside school."

"Who are you kidding, Amy? You really don't care about me. The minute you're out of my sight, you're flirting with somebody."

"What are you talking about? We were having a conference — going over some of Carl's cartoons — and you make it sound as though we were having an orgy."

"It didn't look like a conference to me. More like an excuse for you to be alone with three guys, all of them doing somersaults over you."

"You're wrong, Jeff. I was not flirting, and they were not somersaulting."

"I saw it with my own eyes, so don't tell me I'm wrong."

Before I'd spoken to Jeff, I was ready for an argument, but nothing like this. I could feel tears welling up in my eyes, a combination of anger and hurt, but I tried to keep my voice steady.

"Look, Jeff, I want to be with you, but I also need some space."

"I didn't know I was crowding you."

"I've been trying to be with you whenever I can, even when there are other demands made on me. Like last Saturday, M. J. asked me to go with her to pick out a present for her parents, but I refused because you wanted to be with me all day. I knew you'd get mad if I told you I'd meet you after lunch."

"I never thought I was making 'demands,'

as you call them. If you'd rather do something besides be with me, then you can't care too much about us."

"Because we're going together, doesn't mean we're glued at the hip." I was getting angrier by the minute.

"It's not a question of that. In simple language, I have always made a special effort to arrange my life so that we can spend time together."

"Me, too, but we're not Siamese twins. And I don't like to feel I'm being watched."

"You wouldn't say that if you didn't have something to hide."

"What's that supposed to mean?"

"Don't tell me you don't have a crush on Jerry."

"I don't."

"He was all over you at your so-called conference."

"Well, I do like Jerry, but not *that* way. And I can't help it if he likes me."

"You certainly don't do anything to discourage him."

"I don't have to. He knows you and I are going together — or were." That last remark slipped out, surprising even me, but by then I was too infuriated to take it back.

"I think I'm getting a message from you, Amy. Loud and clear."

"I think you are."

"Then there's no point in continuing — "

"None at all," I said.

I waited for him to say something else, but

51

all I heard was the soft click of the phone. Robotlike, I placed the receiver in its cradle, and sat on the edge of my bed, stunned. I tried to absorb what had happened, and muttered to myself, "It's over, it's over."

I couldn't believe that Jeff and I were finished, that I no longer had a guy, that what I considered the romance of my lifetime had ended. I might have stayed in one position forever if the tears hadn't spilled down my cheeks, forcing me to go into the bathroom for a tissue. I blew my nose, splashed cold water on my face, and stared at my image in the mirror. The last time I'd felt so totally clobbered was a few days before the Junior Prom, and I was sure I'd blown my last chance to be invited. Then Jeff had come along and nothing was the same. I was a different Amy Ross now, more confident, and no longer felt the need to be a chameleon around boys.

I straightened my spine, threw back my shoulders, and tilted my chin up. "You can't let your split with Jeff turn you into a wimp," I said to my face in the mirror. "From now on, you're going to be your own person!"

Having made that vow, I spent the next few hours tossing and turning in bed, trying to figure out how I could adjust to my new status. I finally fell into an exhausted sleep, and woke up feeling like a limp dishrag. I got ready for school in slow motion, and everyone else was sitting at the kitchen table having breakfast when I ambled in.

"Good morning," I muttered, half-heartedly.

"There's some hot cereal on the stove," my mother said.

"You're running late this morning, Aim," my father observed. "I can give you a lift, if you want. You, too, Kenny."

"I'm meeting some kids, right now," Kenny said, getting up. Then he looked at me, dawdling over the stove. "Still in a bad mood?"

"I broke up with Jeff," I said, starting to dish out some cereal. It sounds crazy, but saying those words out loud, announcing our breakup to the world, gave it a finality I wasn't prepared for, and I burst into tears.

"Oh, come on, Amy. You'll get a zillion boyfriends." Kenny was trying to be nice, and that made me cry even harder. I ran out of the kitchen, into my room, and threw myself on the bed. My constrained crying of the previous night was nothing compared to this fresh flood of tears. All the pent-up emotion I'd tried to hold in check was unleashed, and I sobbed uncontrollably. My parents had the good sense to leave me alone, and sure enough, after a few minutes I had cried myself out and knew I had to pull myself together. I looked like an unmade bed, but I dried my eyes, applied some powder and blush-on, and decided I looked normal enough to face the world.

My mother was coming out of her bedroom just as I rushed out of mine.

"Daddy will drive you to school," she said.

"Thanks, Mom." I hurried past her, grateful that she hadn't bugged me with a lot of questions.

My father was waiting for me in the hall, and held the door open. "Bye, dear," he called to my mother.

"Bye, you two," my mother said. Then she added, "You know, Amy, I think Kenny may be right."

I glanced back at her, wondering what she meant. "About what?" I asked.

"About a zillion boyfriends," my father answered for her with a twinkle in his eye.

"You've got to be kidding," I said. But for the first time in what seemed like a century, I was able to smile.

Now that I'd broken the news to my family, it was easier to talk about. I didn't see M. J. until French, and I had to let her know right away. I slipped her a note when eagle-eyed Madam Roget had turned to write something on the blackboard. "*Moi et Jeff — fini!*" my note read. M. J. let out a gasp and looked at me as though she was about to say something, but Madame had turned around, and we knew from experience not to incur her wrath by whispering.

"I'm sorry," M. J. said to me as soon as class was over. "Do you want to tell me what happened?" M. J. is the least nosy person in the world, and that's one of the reasons she's so easy to talk to.

"I'll tell you all at Rico's," I said.

"You mean you want everyone to know, then?"

I nodded my head slowly.

"You sure you don't want to put it on ice awhile, and hope you can get back together?"

"No, I'm afraid that's not possible. And to tell the truth, I'll feel better when the news is out." I didn't add that the sooner everyone knew, the sooner I could start circulating.

Gail and Terry's response to the news was just as I predicted. Gail first expressed shock, then sympathy, but she couldn't resist wanting to know all the details. Terry, as always, was cool and made some remarks about the human condition and the value of experience. They both made me feel better.

The rest of the afternoon we talked about the importance of boys in our lives. Did the Amazon women who subjugated their men know something we didn't? And, was being totally liberated, and therefore independent, so great? After arguing the pros and cons we finally concluded that no matter how hard we tried, no matter how much heartache boys caused, we couldn't live without them.

$\mathcal{S}$even

That old cliché about bad news traveling fast certainly applied to my situation. When I got home from Rico's, Kenny told me the phone had been ringing off the hook — four calls in less than an hour.

"Three boys and one girl," he informed me.

"Thanks, Kenny. Anybody interesting?" I asked.

I hadn't seen Jeff in school all day, and figured we both were avoiding each other. Still, I couldn't suppress the dim hope that maybe he'd called.

"The boys didn't leave their names, and I didn't recognize any of their voices." Kenny, unknowingly, had answered my unspoken question.

"And the girl?"

"Lucy. She left a message. She wants you to phone her as soon as you get in."

56

"I might have guessed," I mumbled. I went into my room and decided I better get my call to her over with.

Lucy is on the chubby side, and doesn't have a terrific complexion. She's very funny and numbers me among her twenty best friends. I like her a lot, but she's a terrible gossip. Although I'm not exactly a saint when it comes to listening to tidbits about other people's love lives, this was the first time I was the one who was being talked about. Lucy would tell me what everyone was saying.

I settled myself on the bed and dialed her number. I was a little nervous about what I might hear, although I'd never known her to be malicious.

"Amy!" she exclaimed, as soon as she heard my voice. "Everybody's talking about it."

"About it," I echoed, inviting her to go on.

"Yes, about you and Jeff. I mean, everyone thought you were the perfect couple. A little too exclusive, maybe, but otherwise, perrr-fect."

"Exclusive," I murmured thoughtfully. "That's probably why it went wrong."

"Well, it did seem that you didn't need anyone else. At least that's what my spies say about Jeff . . . that he only wanted to be alone with you."

"I guess that's true."

"Personally I think that's the most romantic thing I ever heard of!"

"It was pretty romantic."

"Past tense?"

" 'Fraid so."

"That's what I heard today, but I didn't want to spread the word until I heard it from the horse's mouth."

"And I'm the horse, I guess."

"You know, Amy, I'm known as the town crier, but I like to have my facts straight."

"The facts are, Jeff and I are no longer an item."

"And therefore you're free to do whatever you want."

"That's the way I'm trying to look at it."

"It's the only way. In case you didn't know, my brother Charlie heard about you being available and he told me he was going to call you."

"Charlie said that?" I was astonished.

"He's president of the chess club, and I think he might have heard about you from Jeff."

"And he's going to call me?" I couldn't believe it. "I didn't know that Charlie was interested in girls."

"He's shy, that's all, but it doesn't mean he's not interested."

Charlie was the exact opposite of Lucy, except for the fact that they were both pudgy. He was very serious, a world class chess player, and not sociable like his sister. He had a reputation for being very smart, but he was one senior who kept a low profile.

"I would like to get to know him better," I said.

"Great, Amy. I'll pass along the word."

We said good-bye and I hung up, trying to grasp everything Lucy had told me. I'd not been aware that we were considered the "perrrfect couple," but more surprising was hearing that Charlie might be calling me. I could never remember seeing him with a girl, and certainly didn't think of him as a prospective date, but now anything seemed possible. He wasn't my type, but then I hardly knew him. Might as well give him a chance.

I was just about to put the phone back in the hall when it rang again.

"Your line's been busy." It was Jerry's distinctive voice — low and unhurried.

"Yes, it has."

"Are they standing in line already?"

"Could be."

"Well, I hope you're free next Friday. There's a calligraphy show at the Morgan Museum in New York. If we leave right after school, we'll get there before it closes and then we could have dinner."

"Sounds great, but on Fridays — " I cut myself short, because although I'd never missed a Friday at Rico's except when I was in bed with the flu and a-hundred-and-three-degree fever, going out with Jerry suddenly seemed more important.

"Any problem?" Jerry asked.

"No — not at all. I'd love to go with you."

"Fantastic, Amy. I'll see you in school Monday . . . and Tuesday and Wednesday and Thursday . . . and we'll firm up the details."

"Thanks, Jerry. I'm looking forward to it."

"Me, too — more than you know," he said.

I put the receiver down slowly, surprisingly thrilled at the prospect of having a date in New York with Jerry and slightly guilty that I was going to cop out on my girl friends. But I decided I would tell them the truth, and I was sure they would understand. After all, they wouldn't expect me to pass up such an opportunity.

I walked over to my desk and jotted down Jerry's name in the appropriate spot on my calendar. Not that there was any chance I would forget it, but it was satisfying to see his name there. Seconds later, the phone rang again.

"Hi, I hear it's okay to call." It was an unfamiliar boy's voice.

"Who is this?" I asked.

"Oh, it's me, Charlie," he said awkwardly. "I should have identified myself."

"That's okay, Charlie." I tried to put him at ease.

"Umm, I wondered if you wanted to go out?"

Charlie was definitely not accustomed to making dates, and I could tell the whole process was painful for him. He might have been brilliant, but when it came to girls. . . .

"Go out . . . you mean with you?"

"Yes, yes, that's what I mean."

"Well, sure. Did you have something special in mind?"

"N-no, I mean yes. I thought next Saturday we could watch the finals of a chess tournament in Paterson."

"A chess tournament? You mean they have spectators at chess tournaments?"

"Yes, and they're fascinating. You see, I hope to enter some local contests, and this will give me an idea of how they operate. I've only watched them on television, and that's different from being there. What do you say?"

"Why not." Might as well try something new, I thought. "I happen to be free next Saturday."

"You are?"

"Yes, otherwise I wouldn't have accepted."

"Naturally. I should have figured that out."

"What time?"

"I'll pick you up at seven-thirty. Right after dinner."

"Naturally," I said, and tried not to giggle.

"Bye, Amy." I could tell he couldn't wait to end this excruciating conversation.

"Bye," I said, but he'd already hung up and I burst out laughing. Watching a chess match on a Saturday wasn't my idea of heaven, but it was a lot better than staying home and brooding about my lost love.

I wasn't apt to forget my plans with Charlie, but I took the precaution of writing the details — *7:30, Charlie, dress for chess* — in my calendar. Then I took the phone into the hall. It was after six, and I had goofed off as far as helping fix dinner. I knew my family was being indulgent because of the scene I'd created that morning, but I was feeling a lot better now. I was about to offer my services in the kitchen, when the phone rang again.

This time it was Alan, known as the computer nerd of Teaneck High. He had sandy-haired, bland good looks, the nondescript kind that one would expect to see in a modern, sterile corporation. We'd barely exchanged two words in two years, and I couldn't imagine why he'd be calling. But he got right to the point.

"There's going to be an opening of Computerland in the mall in two weeks. I'm going, and I thought you might like to come with me. It'd be a good article for the *Swen*, and you could keep me company."

"Is this a date or an assignment?" I inquired.

"Your choice," he replied somberly.

"I don't know a thing about computers."

"It should be all the more interesting for you then. You'll learn something. Besides, there'll be plenty of food and drink. You can take notes and eat at the same time."

"Sort of like a business lunch."

"You might call it that."

It was obvious that Alan did not have a sense of humor, but that didn't stop me from accepting. Might as well add him to my collection of dates. "I'd like to join you," I said. "When is it?"

"It starts at three-thirty, so we should head for the mall as soon as school is out two weeks from Friday."

"Friday . . . oh dear."

"Don't tell me you're busy."

"Not exactly . . . nothing I can't get out of."

"Good. You see, I thought you'd be the perfect person. I never see you hanging around the computer lab, and I'm interested in your reactions. Plus, you're pretty."

He may have meant that as a compliment, but it came across as though he were describing some high-tech equipment, rather than a flesh-and-blood person.

"All systems go, right?" he asked.

"All systems go," I confirmed, and returned to my room to scribble *Alan, Computerland, 3:30*, in the two weeks from Friday space on my calendar.

I felt a twinge of guilt about not saving the time for M. J., Terry, and Gail. I'd be missing two Fridays in a row. I decided then, that although it might be a little deceptive, I'd wait until the last minute to tell them I couldn't make it the second time. It wasn't that I didn't want to be with them, but I was on a popularity kick, and I wasn't about to do anything to squelch it.

E*ight*

After I finished dinner and helped clean up, I hurried to my room to call M. J. She was just as understanding as I'd hoped about my skipping Rico's.

"You've made a remarkable recovery in twenty-four hours," she joked.

"No point in moping. Besides, I'm sort of making up for lost time."

"What do you mean?"

"I never really went out before Jeff came along. And now, without even trying, I'm getting all these calls."

"That's great, Amy. But don't let it go to your head."

"Course not. I don't really care about any of these guys."

"But there's safety in numbers."

"Something like that. Now I've got to call Gail and Terry, and explain about Friday."

"I'm sure they'll feel the way I do. We'll

miss you, but you've never done it before unless you were sick."

"That's what I think, M. J. And thanks for everything."

I was about to dial Terry's number when the phone rang. Another boy whose voice I didn't recognize.

"Hi, Amy. This is David."

"David — oh . . . hello." I couldn't help sounding surprised because David had never called before. Also, I knew he was going with a girl in the senior class.

"Surprised to hear from me?"

"Sort of."

"I heard you broke up with Jeff, and just last week I split with Cheryl."

"That's too bad." I remembered, then, that Cheryl played violin in the school orchestra, and David was the first cellist. Lucy had once told me that they made beautiful music together.

"Maybe it isn't too bad," David said. "That is, if you'll go to a concert with me next Saturday."

"I'd love to, but I can't. I've already made plans."

"Then how about the following Saturday? There's a series of chamber music concerts at the Y, and I've subscribed for season tickets . . . for two." There was a note of sadness in his voice, and I felt a little sorry for him.

"A week from Saturday would be fine . . .

even though I think I might be playing second fiddle."

"Good," he said, ignoring my attempt at humor. "The quartet is doing a work by Philip Glass. He's a minimalist. I can loan you a book so you can read up on him."

"Uh-huh."

"You don't sound too enthusiastic."

"It's just that I have a lot to do," I said, "and I don't know if I'll have time. Anyhow, I'd love to go with you."

"That's the important thing."

"Maybe it's kismet."

"What do you mean?"

"You know . . . fate. Me splitting with Jeff and you with Cheryl, almost at the exact moment." I couldn't believe I was saying this, but maybe my previously untapped "flirting" resources were surfacing.

"I'll think about that, Amy. But now I've got to go and practice. I've got an audition coming up for Juilliard next month. Have to play before a group of judges, and hope I'll be accepted."

"I don't want to interfere with your career," I joked.

"Don't worry about that," David said with deadly seriousness.

After we said good-bye, I promptly went to my desk and filled in two weeks from Saturday with David's name. Then I called Gail and Terry, and was pleased that they responded just the way M. J. had when I told them about my Friday priority. They both made me feel I was doing the right thing.

It was after nine o'clock by the time I settled down to do my homework. I had several assignments that I couldn't postpone, but I kept glancing at my calendar sprinkled with names of boys — Charlie, Jerry, Alan, and David. I wasn't turned on by any of them, but they were certainly a great way to distract me from thinking about Jeff. And I got this enormous satisfaction in knowing that a year ago I would have killed myself to bone up on their particular interest, and now I was indifferent. For Jerry, I would have pored over art books on calligraphy; I'd have found someone to give me a few private lessons in chess, so that I could impress Charlie; prevail upon Kenny to give me a crash course in computers; read everything I could get my hands on about Philip Glass. It was wonderful not to spend time pursuing subjects that really didn't interest me.

I breezed through my homework — skimming my reading assignments and not bothering to double check my answers in math. Fortunately I had a good track record in my academic subjects and could occasionally get by without working too hard. I just wasn't in the mood to study!

I took my time taking a bubble bath, then splashed myself with cologne, and brushed my hair until it glistened. Next, I dug out of my bottom drawer the delicate sateen and lace nightshirt that my grandmother, Mumsie, had given to me for my sixteenth birthday. It was shell pink, and so fragile-looking that I'd kept it in piles of tissue paper and never worn it. But I had this strange impulse to be glamorous, so I tuned in my radio to a program that played only romantic dance music, and I waltzed around the room, straightening up, frequently glancing at myself in the mirror, and in the process unleashing a lot of pent-up emotional energy.

Suddenly I felt very tired and collapsed on my bed. I'd managed not to dwell on Jeff for long periods of time. I'd gone all day without thinking about him more than every other hour. But because it was so late, and I was exhausted, I found myself missing him terribly.

Forget it, an inner voice said. *It's over*. I got up, pulled down the spread, and out of habit folded it neatly at the foot of my bed. Then I turned off the radio, and was about to flick off the overhead light, when what seemed like an inexplicable force pulled me to my desk. There, as if to reassure me, was my calendar with the names of Charlie, Jerry, Alan, and David staring me in the face. "This is only the beginning," I murmured. "Remember, you're a new you, Amy Ross."

The following Friday, Jerry had arranged to drive to school so that we could leave as soon as the final bell rang. I had dressed carefully in a red plaid skirt, dark red flats, and a cotton long-sleeved blouse. I wore a thin gold chain and button earrings. I considered wearing a dress to school, but that would have invited too many questions. It was strange enough that I wasn't in my usual jeans and running shoes.

Since I was missing out on Rico's, I made a special effort to have lunch with M. J., Terry, and Gail. They told me I looked perfect for viewing calligraphy and going out to dinner in New York. "Ladylike but not boring," is how Terry summed up my appearance. It was a great send-off from my friends.

At first Jerry and I talked about the *Swen* and future stories we might do, but he soon switched the topic of conversation to himself. He couldn't decide whether he wanted to be a teacher on the college level one day, or go into business with his uncle, who had a successful real estate firm. But first he wanted to earn some money so that he could bum around Europe.

I soon discovered that although Jerry was pleasant enough, he was only interested in himself. By the time we arrived at Thirty-Sixth Street and parked the car around the corner from the museum, I had heard his life's story — and he hadn't asked me one word about myself. Maybe later, I thought.

The calligraphy collection was unique, and

included an exhibition of illuminated manuscripts done in the Middle Ages. It surprised me that Jerry seemed less interested than I, since it was his idea. He was impatient to leave, but I insisted on lingering over some of the more fascinating displays.

Then he asked whether I wanted Chinese or Japanese food. Instead of finding out what he preferred — the old Amy — I promptly told him Chinese. The fact that I knew my own mind seemed to please him.

We drove to a restaurant in Chinatown that he knew about and pigged out on a variety of exotic dishes. Jerry continued to tell me his hopes and dreams, and we were practically home before he got around to asking about me. I had just begun to tell him about how I planned to be a writer, probably of fiction, when he put his arm around me and interrupted.

"You're really pretty, Amy," he said.

"Thank you," I said, slightly taken aback. I appreciated the compliment, but he was obviously totally uninterested in what I was saying. He parked the car in front of my house.

The next thing I knew, he had folded his arms around me and kissed me on the mouth. I didn't mind him giving me a good-night kiss, but I didn't want it to go beyond that.

"What's wrong?" he asked, as I pulled away from him.

"Nothing. It's just that this is enough for now."

"Does that mean that next time I'll be allowed *two* good-night kisses?"

"Who knows?" I was secretly pleased that there would be a next time, and I hadn't even tried.

"You're something else, Amy," he said, smiling at me. "You're really something else."

N^{ine}

The following morning at eight-thirty the phone awakened me. I buried my head under the pillow, sure that it wasn't for me. There's an unwritten law that none of my friends calls one another, upon penalty of death, before ten o'clock on the weekends. I was about to doze off when Kenny charged into my room, dragging the phone with him.

"It's for you," he shouted, dumping the phone on the floor beside my bed. Then, in a lower voice, "It's a boy."

I stretched out my arm and Kenny handed me the receiver.

"Sorry I woke you, Amy, but I —"

"Who is this?" I was still half asleep and not thinking too clearly.

"Don't tell me you've forgotten already."

"Oh, it's you, Jerry."

"I'm so happy you remembered," he said. "I fell asleep thinking about you, and I woke up thinking about you, and I couldn't wait to call."

"Uh-huh."

"I wondered if there's an outside chance that you're free tonight. There's a new Eddie Murphy movie at the Lyceum. I can't get the car again, but we could take the bus."

"Can't, I'm busy."

"How about next weekend?"

" 'Fraid not."

"Are you trying to tell me something?"

"No, not at all." I sat up, fully awake now, aware that Jerry might be getting the wrong idea. "I mean I have plans for Friday and Saturday, but I really do want to go out with you."

"How about the Saturday after?"

"That would be great."

"I'll call you later, and we'll make a definite plan. But don't forget to pencil me in."

"Don't worry," I said, and sank back on my pillow.

I was about to doze off when the phone rang again. I fumbled around on the floor, and halfway out of the bed picked up the receiver.

"Hello," I croaked in an upside-down position.

"Are you all right?" It was Charlie.

"I'm fine, but isn't it awfully early?"

"Wanted to remind you about tonight, in case you forgot or something."

"How could I?" I asked, thinking I was getting good at this game of not saying quite what I meant. "Besides, I've got you in my book."

"In your book? Are you writing a book?"

"No," I groaned, trying to hide my exasperation. "That's just an expression. It means I've got you on my calendar, which is also my engagement book."

"Oh sure, sure. I'll see you later."

"Later," I said, and managed to extricate myself from the telephone cord and dive under the covers.

I loved getting phone calls, but I also needed some sleep. Mumsie, who cares much more about looks than my mother, is always giving me these little beauty tips. She firmly believes that "beauty" sleep occurs before midnight, wards off wrinkles, and keeps eyes sparkling. I'd never thought too much about looks, but now that my antennae were up for boys, it seemed dumb not to heed her advice. Not that I felt the tiniest need to do anything for Charlie, but one of Mumsie's admonitions was, "You'll never know who you'll see."

Actually, I thought it might be amusing to look different, as long as I had a new status. After sleeping another hour, I called M. J. and asked her if she thought I should go punk or sophisticated.

"What are you talking about, Amy?" She sounded as though I had flipped out.

"I feel like doing something different," I explained. "And you're so good at fixing hair, I thought maybe you'd do mine in a new style."

"You're not the punk type — green and purple spikes."

"I wasn't about to go that far. But how about a French twist?"

"That's a possibility. Who are you trying to impress?"

"Certainly not Charlie. Besides, I don't think he'd notice the difference."

"Come over for lunch, and we'll experiment."

"Great."

"And you can tell me all about last night, and Jerry."

"Not much to tell, except he's a lot more self-centered than I thought. The important thing is, he's asked me out again."

"That really means a lot to you, doesn't it?"

"You're the one who told me there was safety in numbers."

"But you wouldn't lead boys on if you didn't like them, would you?"

"I might," I admitted. "It's a good way not to get hurt."

"I think the important thing is to be true to yourself."

"You're not going to give me a lecture," I said, and laughed a little so that I didn't sound so irritable.

"Course not," she answered quickly. But we both knew I was on the defensive, and the last thing I wanted to do was get into a fight with my best friend.

* * *

I spent the entire afternoon at M. J.'s playing hairdresser and giggling, and I went home with my hair wrapped in a twist. I didn't feel at all like me, and M. J. said she was indulging me in a temporary lapse, and hoped I would return to normalcy in twenty-four hours.

"I will," I promised, "if for no other reason than that I couldn't possibly manage this style by myself, and my mother would never have the patience."

"I really like you *au naturel*, although you do look quite chic," M. J. appraised me.

"It takes guts to do something different," I defended myself, knowing she didn't really like the results.

"Promise you won't tell anyone I'm responsible."

"Promise," I said. "And I better get home before I lose my nerve."

Kenny was the first one to see me. He was wheeling his bike into the garage just as I was coming into the house.

"What have you done?" he shouted. "You look crazy."

"How would you know?" I countered, and escaped into the house before I could hear his answer.

My parents were in the den, where my mother was working on her hooked rug and my father was having a beer.

"What happened to your hair?" my father asked. He looked at me curiously.

"It's a French twist," I said as evenly as possible.

He was about to say something else, but I noticed my mother shoot him one of her "Be quiet" looks.

"It's fun to try something new," she said.

"That's what I think." I resisted adding, "Especially when I don't feel I have to please anybody but me."

I felt very self-conscious all through dinner, although no further remarks were made about my coiffure. I was sure my mother had warned my father and brother to leave me alone.

When Charlie picked me up, he was so uncomfortable saying hello to my folks that he didn't really notice me until we got into his car.

"There's something different about you," he commented.

"My hair," I explained.

He looked at me as though he were seeing me for the first time, and after a moment he said, "I like it."

I was so happy that someone had responded positively — no matter how much I pretended not to care — that I said, "You have excellent taste, Charlie."

"No one ever said that before."

"They just didn't notice, I guess," I said.

"You know, Lucy said I'd like you . . . and I do already." He revved up the motor, and I settled back in my seat.

Another conquest, I thought, and I hadn't even been trying!

All the way to Paterson, Charlie told me the fundamentals of chess, and that the objective was to checkmate the opposing king. He was totally absorbed in his subject but I couldn't get into it. The one fact that grabbed me was that there could be as much as an hour between moves.

"Is that apt to happen tonight?"

"It could."

I nodded my head, wondering how I could get through the evening without falling asleep.

We found a place to park the car on the street across from the community center where the match was to take place. There were well over a hundred people milling around the corridor, and I was astounded that so many people were interested in watching chess. Charlie produced passes that allowed us to enter an enormous room that could have been a gymnasium or a ballroom, and for the occasion had been converted into an auditorium. It was filled with folding chairs that faced a stage where the players would appear. Above the stage was an electric board that would show the moves.

"I can't believe there are so many kids here," I said.

"There's one kid, Jacob Tessrin, who's playing. He's fifteen years old and he's a phenom. He's won all the high school championships. He's playing a thirty-five-year-old lawyer who's known for his steady, if not brilliant, game."

There were fifteen minutes until the match would begin and we found some seats on the center aisle. Charlie was going on about the famous world chess championship in Moscow between Karpov, thirty-three years old, and Kasparov, twenty-one, the youngest person ever to compete in a title match.

"It was the longest drawn-out draw in championship history. Karpov was ahead, but hanging in by a thread because he was physically and mentally exhausted. Then, probably because the referee favored Karpov, he arbitrarily stopped the match. . . ."

I was only half listening to what Charlie was saying, because in all honesty I wasn't too interested. Then suddenly, I involuntarily let out a gasp. Charlie undoubtedly thought I was responding to his story, but actually I was reacting to seeing Jeff. Our paths hadn't crossed since our last devastating conversation. I'd avoided going to the library when I knew he might be there, and if he did happen to see me in the halls or the cafeteria, he never let me know. But now, when I least expected it, he was going down the aisle, and taking a seat three rows ahead of us. He was wearing a dark red sweater over an open-necked blue shirt, and he looked particularly good.

Then, to my dismay, I noticed he wasn't alone. He was following a girl who I recognized as Sally Straus, a blond-haired, blue-eyed tenth-grader I hardly knew, but I could tell she thought she was the bee's knees. They sat down and she started talking animatedly to Jeff, who was hanging on to every word. I felt angry and annoyed, but I couldn't take my eyes off them. Charlie didn't notice how distracted I was as he elaborated on the Russian match.

"Kasparov held the champion through a record seventeen straight draws, until Karpov won his fifth game. He needed only one more to win the title. But Kasparov gathered momentum, and four draws later won his first game. Karpov is said to have lost fifteen pounds through this ordeal, and he started to make blunders. He was going into a tailspin, and the game was stopped. That means Karpov remains champion. Isn't that incredible?"

"Incredible," I muttered, although I hadn't registered one word.

Then the players appeared, Jacob wearing jeans and a T-shirt, and the lawyer dressed in a three-piece suit. They bowed slightly to the audience, which gave them a welcoming round of applause, and then seated themselves at the chess table.

I tried hard to watch the electric board, and not stare at the back of Jeff's head. But after the first few moves, I gave up. The game didn't make sense to me, although Charlie seemed transfixed.

A zillion questions ran through my mind: Was it my imagination, or was Jeff holding her hand? Had he been taking out Sally regularly, or was this the first time? Wasn't it strange that he would choose a tenth-grader? Whom could I ask about her without sounding jealous?

The match was tied at two all, and this was the deciding game. I knew if there was a draw, it might go on forever. I was increasingly anxious for the evening to end so that I could get away from Jeff and Sally. I wanted to escape without them seeing me, mainly because I wasn't sure how I would react. I didn't want to give Jeff the satisfaction of seeing me lose my cool.

The match lasted more than two hours — a painfully long time, it seemed to me — but finally it was over. Jacob Tessrin was the winner, and the crowd cheered warmly as the lights brightened and the players shook hands.

"That guy's brilliant, absolutely brilliant. I'll explain his strategy to you on the way home," Charlie said.

"Then we better get started." I stood up and began hurrying up the aisle.

"What's the big rush?" Charlie asked, as I threaded my way through the crowd.

"I was getting a little claustrophobic." That wasn't a total lie if you define claustrophobia as a need to get away from a confined space.

"There's an ice cream shop a couple blocks away. We could get some air and a cone."

"Terrific." I was sure Jeff wouldn't be going there. He preferred going to Rico's or the Pizza Palace.

For the next hour I was deluged with information about knights, bishops, rooks, and pawns. All the time Charlie was talking I was thinking about Jeff and Sally, and it suddenly dawned on me that Sally might be a member of the chess club. When Charlie finished describing Tessrin's final coup, I asked casually, "Are there any famous women players?"

"There's a girl from Hungary, Susan Polgar, who at the age of eleven won the world's under-sixteen chess championship. At twelve, she was the only female entrant and won an international tournament in Bulgaria. Now she's fifteen, and is the highest-rated female chess player in the world. She insists on entering male tournaments, although that has been frowned on by the Hungarian Chess Federation."

"That's amazing," I said, but wanted to get back to my original point. "How about the chess club at school? Any girls?"

"There are a few, but only one is any good."

"Who is she?"

"Sally Straus. She's a terrific player. Just joined this year and she's only a tenth-grader."

"Must be smart."

"Good at chess. That's all I know."

I was dying to find out more, but even Charlie might get suspicious.

"I'm good at Trivial Pursuit," I said. I knew it was an absurd remark, but I was feeling competitive with Sally.

"What's that got to do with anything?"

"Nothing. Just that you can't be good at everything."

"Guess not." If Charlie thought I was sounding ridiculous, he was polite enough not to say so.

When we arrived at my house, he walked me to the door, and then shook my hand. It wasn't the usual way to end an evening, but it suited me perfectly.

"I hope you'll go out with me again, Amy."

"I'd like that," I said.

"I'll call you then, okay?" He started to back away.

"I wish you would," I said, and opened the door. When I turned to wave good-bye, he was already out of sight.

I closed the door and thought that even if he invited me to a cricket match — the only game I can think of more boring to watch than chess — I was going to say yes. If Jeff was going out with girls — or worse yet, one girl — I needed all the dates I could get!

I put on my night shirt, washed my face, brushed my teeth, and saw that my French twist was unraveling. It felt good to take out the pins and let my hair fall loose. I wondered what Jeff would have said if he'd seen me looking so sophisticated. What difference does it make? I thought, as I combed out the remaining evidence of M. J.'s creation. I've got to will myself to stop thinking about Jeff and focus on next weekend, which meant Alan and David.

Ten

All week I put off telling my friends that I wouldn't be at Rico's again. By the time Friday rolled around, I still hadn't said anything. Then Friday morning, I had no choice. When I arrived at school, Terry, Gail, and M. J. were having an intense conversation. Gail caught my eye, and waved me over to where they were standing on the school steps. The first bell had just rung, which meant we had five minutes.

"Don't have time now, Amy, but I'll tell you at Rico's about what I might be doing over Christmas."

I took a deep breath and spluttered, "Tell me now. I can't make Rico's today."

"Two times in a row!" Gail shouted.

"What's it this time? Prince Andrew in town?" Terry asked languidly.

M. J. didn't say anything, which made me really uncomfortable. It wasn't like me not to confide in her, and she was justifiably hurt.

"I'm going to the opening of Computerland. There might be a story there for the *Swen*, and I think it's time for me to learn something about word processors, if I'm going to be a serious writer, and —"

"Who're you going with?" Gail interrupted. She, as well as the others, knew that the real reason I wouldn't be at Rico's was because of a boy.

"Alan — he's interested in the reactions of someone who's *not* a computer freak."

"You couldn't go tomorrow, or next week? It's still going to be there, you know." Normally, I appreciated Gail's outspokenness, but now I wished she'd shown a little restraint.

"He didn't ask me for tomorrow, or next week. Besides, if there's a story there for the *Swen*, I should cover the opening."

The three of them looked at me skeptically, which was worse than accusing me of fudging the truth. Then, mercifully, the bell rang and we hurried up the stairs to avoid the crunch.

I wasn't sure if it was by design or coincidence, but the rest of the day I hardly exchanged two words with M. J., Gail, or Terry. During lunch, Carl cornered me as I stood in the cafeteria line and asked me to sit with him.

"I've got an idea I want to discuss with you, since you're the feature editor."

"Sure." I hadn't seen my friends, so they couldn't accuse me of avoiding them.

I paid for my lunch, and followed him to a corner table. As soon as we sat down, he told me about a comic strip character he had invented, named "Walnuts."

"It's okay, if it's not just a spin-off of *Peanuts*."

"Not the least like *Peanuts*. See here." He pulled out of his portfolio some preliminary sketches depicting various poses of Walnuts, a curly-topped, wide-eyed character, with an endearing smile.

"He's adorable," I said.

"And the background will be Teaneck High, not elementary school. No chance of me being accused of ripping off someone else's idea."

"Then I think we should run a whole series."

"I've been working on a couple of strips. They're in the *Swen* office. Maybe you'll meet me there after school, and help me decide which one I should present to the staff meeting next week."

"I'd like to, but I have other plans."

"How about tomorrow?"

"Tomorrow's Saturday," I said.

"That's right."

"School's closed."

"I'm asking you out, Amy."

"You are?" I was astounded. Carl was known as a loner, only interested in his art.

"When can I see you — and I don't mean in school."

"Any weekend that I'm free. Not this one, though."

"I'll call you. Maybe you can fit me in somewhere between now and Christmas."

"I'm sure there's a place for you." I could be just as quick with the repartee as he.

"You are a provocative one, Amy."

Just at that moment, Jerry walked over to where we were sitting. "Is this an editorial conference, and why wasn't I invited?" he asked.

"I was asking Amy's opinion about Walnuts."

"You're sure that's all, Carl?"

"Not sure at all."

"Just remember, I saw her first." Jerry was smiling, but there was an undercurrent of seriousness in his voice.

"It's a free country, Jerry." Carl smiled wryly, and I sensed that beneath the banter, they were competing for me. It was a new sensation, and I didn't mind at all.

Computerland was so bewildering I was actually a little embarrassed that I'd even entertained the idea of writing an article about it. Since I didn't know a PIP program from a CP/M, or a byte from a MITE, I was completely lost.

Alan was bug-eyed as we went from one exhibit to another. From time to time he remembered I was with him and would point out some special features of new programs. It didn't bother him that I didn't know what he was talking about.

He insisted that we stop at one of the booths where a representative was talking up his company's new material.

"Wasn't he fantastic?" Alan exclaimed after the lecture. "Did you hear him say that the 'Short Hand' program allows the user to redefine as many as thirty-six keys on the computer?"

"Really."

"And it can zap out with one keystroke a whole block of text."

"No kidding."

"And the Print Buffer On-Line enables users to set aside as much as 62,000 bytes of data as a print buffer so that the computer can move the other tasks while waiting for the printer to catch up."

I muffled a yawn but Alan didn't notice and went right on talking. We wandered around two more hours, which felt more like two days, and then an announcement came over the loudspeaker telling everyone in computerese language that we must "abandon," "save," "exit," and "return." There was a lot of chuckling, and I happily surmised that the place was closing and we had to leave.

Alan asked me if I'd like to go to the Pizza Palace. I hesitated a moment, remembering the many times Jeff and I had gone there after the movies, or after a party, just so we could be by ourselves and put off leaving each other.

"If you don't want to . . ." Alan began.

"No . . . yes. I mean, sure."

We walked the several blocks to the Pizza Palace, during which time Alan must have pressed some inner command button that gave me his undivided attention.

"What did you think, Amy?"

"I didn't understand it."

"You're not interested in learning anymore?"

"Not really."

"I can't believe it!" We walked along in silence for a while as he did his best to absorb what I had just confessed. Then he said brightly, "Maybe you'd like to come to an Introduction to Computers seminar that's scheduled every Saturday at Teaneck Tech. It's for people like you, who don't know anything."

My instinctive reaction was to say no, I'd already had more information than I could cope with. But something stopped me. It was a way of guaranteeing a date on a Saturday night, and if nothing better came along. . . .

"That might be a good idea," I said.

"Good, Amy. I'll call you and we'll firm something up. But I think you should be a little better prepared, so let me tell you some of the basics."

We had arrived at the Pizza Palace and I followed Alan to a table in the back of the restaurant that I had shared so many times with Jeff. There were so many memories, and they all came back to me in a rush.

"The first thing you should know is how to format a disk."

"Format a disk," I repeated, trying to concentrate on what Alan was saying.

"Yes, that's absolutely necessary. A new diskette must be magnetically formatted to prepare it to receive information that you input."

"Of course," I said. But I knew I was a lost cause. I couldn't care less about disks and formatting.

"And you must copy all your master diskettes as a precautionary measure. The copy becomes your working disk and you don't have to worry about anything bad happening to it because you always have a backup."

"The only thing I can see to worry about is people. I can't see worrying about a machine."

"But you're a writer, and writers love word processors."

"Not all. I read an interview with Kurt Vonnegut. He wouldn't dream of using one."

"He's the exception."

"And so am I."

Alan, for the moment, was speechless. I wasn't being disagreeable on purpose, just saying what I believed. I went on:

"I think there's a connection between the pen and the brain. Even the typewriter can get in the way."

"You're very interesting, Amy." Alan looked at me admiringly. "I never heard that point of view, but I hope it doesn't mean you won't come to a computing seminar with me."

"Of course not," I assured him. "I still have an open mind."

Although what I was thinking was, I might have an open Saturday. Being popular meant being busy on the weekend. I couldn't tolerate not having a date every Saturday night, even if I ran the risk of dying of boredom.

Eleven

The concert at the Y was a treat, especially compared to my ordeal at the chess match and in Computerland. I do love music, including classical, and I even enjoyed the Philip Glass piece, which I thought was amusing. They also played the "Trout" quintet by Schubert, which is one of my favorites. It was performed by a guest pianist and a double bass player who were very well known. They finished with the Dvorak quintet, which I happened to be familiar with, and I thought the whole program was beautiful.

When the performers were finished, the audience stood up and gave them a standing ovation. "Fantastic," I said to David, while I applauded enthusiastically.

"Yeah, it wasn't bad," he conceded.

"Wasn't bad?" I thought he must be the only one there who wasn't enthralled.

"I'll tell you about it as soon as we get out

of here. Would you like to go to Rico's?"

"Sure," I said, thinking I might as well get used to going places where I'd gone regularly with Jeff.

As soon as we left the auditorium and began walking toward the restaurant, David began his analysis. By the time we'd reached Rico's, I felt I had the equivalent of at least a half semester of Music Appreciation. He was particularly eloquent in discussing Philip Glass, whom he described as "the quintessential minimalist, sounding repetitive, but actually taking a single theme and making infinitesimally small changes."

We had arrived at Rico's, taken a seat in a back booth, ordered a couple of Tabs, and David was still going strong on the subject of minimalism. I refused to let his dissertation take the edge off the glow I was still feeling from the concert, and I finally interrupted.

"I loved the 'Trout.' It's so melodic."

"I was in a terrific group that played it quite differently. I liked our interpretation better."

"It really grabbed me."

"They took the second movement much too fast, to say nothing of the stilted phrasing."

"I didn't notice. Seemed perfect to me."

"Then you probably didn't see that the cellist's bowing left something to be desired."

"I guess you'd know, since it is your instrument." I was beginning to see the futility of trying to get across my opinion.

"I started playing at seven years old with a half-sized cello."

"No kidding," I said.

"My parents made me practice, but I didn't mind. I had a natural aptitude."

"I had a chance to take lessons," I said, "but I didn't want to take the time to practice. Probably because I *don't* have a natural aptitude."

"Probably." It was the first time he'd agreed with me.

"Well, I really love music, but I guess I'll always be a listener."

"We artists need listeners." He looked pleased, totally unaware of his arrogance, and I bit my lip to keep from laughing.

"I always enjoy the school concerts," I told him.

"Then you'll really want to go to the next one. I'm playing the Dvorak cello concerto. I just hope the orchestra's good enough to handle the accompaniment."

"That *must* be a problem," I said with mock seriousness.

He nodded his head, not for a moment realizing that I was putting him on. In fact, my response only succeeded in encouraging him to talk about himself even more. He told me that in the spring he would be auditioning for Juilliard, one of the world's leading music conservatories. He now spent all his free time preparing one classical and one romantic piece, which he would play before a jury of three.

"From what you tell me, David, you don't need to worry."

"Probably not, but I can't be too careful."

He expounded on the necessity of mastering technique so that he could play with more emotion. My eyes were beginning to glaze over and I wasn't unhappy when he said he thought we should leave.

"Tomorrow's Sunday," he explained, "and it's my best day to practice. If I don't get enough sleep, my fingers don't seem to work properly."

We paid the bill, and made our way to the door. On the way out, I caught a glimpse of Sally Straus, sitting in a front booth and smiling at whoever was sitting opposite her. I was afraid to look, and afraid not to. I just had to know if she was with Jeff.

David was already waiting for me at the door, so I had to make a quick decision. I knew it would be totally rude, as well as foolish, to turn around and stare. But I was tempted to do just that when I heard Sally's silvery laugh, and then her voice: "Oh, Jeff, you really are so cute."

I was glad the place was dimly lit so that no one could see how red my face had become. David was holding the door open for me. I brushed past him, took several deep breaths of the cool night air, and tried to calm down.

David came up to me then, suspecting

nothing, and put his arm around my shoulder. "You're such a good listener, Amy. I hope we can see each other again."

"That's a good idea, David." That wasn't a lie, I told myself. More than ever I needed to keep busy, to keep my mind off Jeff and Sally, to find someone new to care about. Maybe one of these dates would develop into something resembling a romance. If nothing else, I thought rather grimly, I've acquired a lot of new information. And at the rate I'm going, I'll get a zillion invites to the Senior Prom.

But no matter how hard I tried, I could never get Jeff out of my mind. Every time I came home from a date, whether it was dining at a French restaurant, or seeing a terrific performer, or watching an exciting sports event, I knew I would rather have been alone with Jeff — doing nothing — than living it up with someone I didn't care about. Although I had trouble admitting it even to myself, he still meant more to me than any glittering social life. Often I fantasized about him calling me, and saying that he wanted to get back together. There was never a night that I didn't fall asleep thinking about him.

Then one day even my fantasy was destroyed. For weeks I hadn't had time to read any new fiction, which was one of my favorite pastimes. I thought I'd make up for it and take three books out at once, which was the rule for recently published books. After my last class, I hurried to the library, and went down the center aisle to the Recent Books shelf, which was located at the far end of the room. I was thinking so hard about what books I might take out that I almost crashed into Jeff, who had approached from the side.

"Oh," I gulped, "it's you."

"Oh," he said, looking just as amazed as I felt.

I was totally unprepared, but I had to say something — something to let him know I hadn't stopped caring about him. But I had too much pride to come out and say just that. Maybe I could drop a hint, let him know he was still on my mind.

"I've wanted to talk to you," I began.

"You have? What about?" He looked kind of pleased, but I wasn't too sure.

I wanted to tell him that I hadn't stopped loving him, but I didn't have the nerve.

"About life and stuff." That was about as much as I could say.

There was this awful silence, then finally Jeff spoke. "What have you been doing?"

Unfortunately, my answer unintentionally reminded him of our last confrontation. "I've been doing my thing. . . ."

"That's what I supposed."

"The *Swen* takes a lot of time."

"I guess so."

"Also, I'm still on the volleyball team."

"And I understand you have a heavy social schedule."

"I do like to keep busy, Jeff, don't you?"

"Sure."

Our conversation was going nowhere, Jeff was unbending as ever, and this unexpected meeting was getting increasingly painful. I thought I'd give it one last try.

"Jeff, I still . . . I still. . . ." I almost came out and said, "I still love you," but something stopped me. "I'm still an individual, and you can't really accept that."

"It doesn't mean that I don't . . . I don't. . . ."

"Don't what?"

"Don't care about you. But I can't help being the way I am, Amy."

"Me neither, Jeff."

We simultaneously turned toward the shelf as though we knew we had come to an impasse. Then the warning bell sounded, which meant we had only seven minutes before the library closed. It was hardly enough time to choose discriminately, but I didn't care. My eyes had misted over, and I had trouble reading the titles anyway. I grabbed three off the shelf and mumbled something about having to get home. The last thing in the world I wanted was to have Jeff see me go to pieces.

At least, I thought, I know where I stand. I had been close enough to touch him, and I knew he was still the only boy for me. With just one bit of encouragement, I would have been willing to try again. But I had to be my own person, and if he couldn't accept that, everything was hopeless. If nothing else, my unexpected meeting with Jeff just reinforced my need to be the belle of Teaneck High.

My wish to be popular was being fulfilled beyond my wildest dreams. For the next couple of months, I was swept up in a social whirlwind. There weren't enough Fridays and Saturdays to accommodate all the boys who wanted to take me out. My solution to that problem was to make Sunday afternoon another time that I could have a date.

Often, my parents would plan something special on Sundays for the whole family, but I managed to get out of it. One Sunday my father was taking Kenny to an automobile show at the Coliseum in Manhattan, and my mother asked me to visit Mumsie with her in New York City. Mumsie was recovering from a cold, and she told my mother she was feeling neglected, and specifically wanted to see me.

Mumsie lives in an old-world building on the Upper East Side and normally I would consider it a treat to see her. She always spoils me to death, and it's obvious I'm her favorite grandchild. But this particular Sunday I had made plans with a new guy, Preston, who was considered Teaneck High's "best-looking senior." He had a reputation for taking out a girl once and then dumping her. I considered him a challenge. I didn't know if I liked him or not, but I was curious to see if I could break the pattern.

It was Sunday morning, and Kenny came barreling into my room.

"Wake up, Amy! It's ten-thirty and everything's ready. You're going to get burned pancakes if you don't hurry."

"I'd like to skip brunch today," I mumbled. "I'm meeting Preston at twelve and he's taking me out to lunch and to some Off-Off Broadway play."

"Uh-oh. I'm in trouble."

I rubbed my eyes and squinted at him. "Why are you in trouble?"

"Because the messenger who bears the bad news gets killed. Didn't you know that?"

"Are you trying to tell me something?" I asked.

"In a way. Dad just said he'd like to know if he had a daughter living here or just a boarder."

"I hear what you're saying," I said, and dragged myself out of bed, threw on a robe, washed up quickly, and flew into the dining room where everyone was already seated. I felt a little bit like an intruder, and my father's greeting didn't help.

"It's nice that you're honoring us with your presence," he said.

I laughed a little nervously, not sure whether he was being funny. "Got home late."

"For a change," he muttered. He was definitely not being funny!

101

"Dad and I are going to the auto show, Amy. Isn't that neat?" Kenny knew what was going on, and was helping me out.

"Neat," I murmured.

"I thought you'd come visit Mumsie with me. She hasn't seen you in ages, and she's staying in because of her cold," my mother said. "We could all drive in together."

"Can't today. I'm being picked up in an hour and I can't break a date at the last minute." I poured syrup over my pancakes and made a feeble attempt to eat them.

"Now I know the answer," my father said. "I do have a boarder living here."

I pretended I didn't know what he meant and was grateful when everyone had finished eating, so I could clear away the dishes, and escape. My father would get over what was bothering him, and I had to get ready to meet Preston. As for Mumsie, she'd been nursing her cold for two weeks. She really didn't have to act like an invalid in order to get attention!

Twelve

I couldn't wait for Greg to come home for the Christmas holidays, but unfortunately he arrived in the late afternoon on a Friday, and I was on my way out. All I could do was give him a bear hug and tell him I'd talk to him later. I had a date with Preston for the third time, which meant I'd broken all records, and I didn't want to risk losing him. Not that Preston did much for me. Besides a handsome face, he had very little to recommend him. On a scale of one to ten, he was a plus ten for looks, but his personality hovered around a minus two. However, I enjoyed adding him to my roster of boys.

The problem was that Greg was only home for ten days, and I was busier than ever. I was present at our annual egg nog party with our neighbors, I exchanged presents with all the members of my family, and I sat next to Mumsie at our traditional Christmas dinner, but the truth was I was always anxious to split. Greg and Kenny had plans, too, but they didn't have every minute accounted for the way I did.

In addition to my regular dates, there were lots of holiday parties. It was inevitable that I would bump into Jeff at some of the bigger bashes. He was just as reluctant as I to make contact, but I couldn't resist checking out who he was escorting. On three different occasions, there was no question that it was Sally. She was the only girl I ever saw him dancing with, and that was all I needed to reinforce my determination to be a social butterfly.

Two days before Greg was to fly back to Maine, he literally blocked the door as I was about to leave the house.

"Hello," he said, "my name is Greg and I'd like to introduce myself. I've caught glimpses of you occasionally, and I thought it would be nice if we met."

"Greg, I'm in a hurry. Supposed to meet Carl in five minutes at the mall and I'm already late."

Greg didn't budge, just looked at his watch and said, "It's now eleven A.M. In less than forty-eight hours I will be flying back to Maine and we haven't had more than a three-minute conversation since I arrived."

"I didn't plan it that way. It just happened. And now is not the right time." I couldn't keep a shrill note out of my voice.

"When is the right time? Do I have to make an appointment to see my sister?"

"Don't be ridiculous. Can't we talk about this later?" I started to reach behind him for the door knob, but he wasn't giving an inch.

"Look, Amy, I know you're busy, but it would be nice if you'd relax a little. You're on some kind of merry-go-round, and eventually you've got to slow down."

"Are you suggesting I should stay home every minute?"

"Hardly. All I'm suggesting is that you think about somebody else once in a while," he said.

"Don't tell me you're going to pull the 'big brother' act on me. I've managed to survive without it ever since you went away."

"If that's how you feel. . . ." He slowly moved away from the door, allowing me to pass.

"That's how I feel," I said breezily, and rushed out.

As I hurried along, I tried to convince myself that Greg was being oversensitive, maybe even a little envious of my social life. But that didn't make sense. He had plenty of friends, both boys and girls, and he'd always backed me up in the past.

Then I remembered how he'd helped me learn to play the guitar last year, so I could impress some boy at school; and how, when I was feeling my most desperate about getting a bid to the Junior Prom, he'd actually

offered to have me go with him and his gang
— the most humiliating thing I could think
of, although the kindest invitation I'd ever
had; and most of all, how much fun we'd
always had just talking.

Well, I thought, people change, and now
he just doesn't understand me. The best thing
I could do would be to forget about his broth-
erly advice.

I realized I was really late, so I started
running rapidly to make up for lost time.
Also, I wanted to blot out my conversation
with Greg. Carl was taking me to a small
gallery where there was an exhibition of
wood prints, and I tried to concentrate on
that. I'd been looking forward to it, and there
was no point in letting my brother ruin my
whole day. I ran even faster, trying hard to
erase from my mind everything he'd said. By
the time I'd reached the mall, I'd almost been
successful. But it wasn't so easy to ignore the
lump in my throat.

I didn't really talk to Greg again before he
left for college. The few times we might have
had even a casual conversation at the breakfast table, he acted as though I wasn't there.

My parents and Kenny were going to drive
him to the airport, and apparently it didn't
occur to him to ask me to join them. The
assumption that I already had plans was correct. I shouldn't have been offended, but it
wouldn't have killed Greg to invite me along.

I literally bumped into him the day he was

to leave. He was toting his suitcase out of his room, and I was rushing into the hall.

"You're leaving, Greg."

"You guessed it."

"Aren't you going to say good-bye?"

"Oh, that's an idea. Good-bye, Amy."

"Maybe I'll write you, or something."

"Maybe you will." He didn't even smile as he hurried past me.

"Come on, Greg," Kenny yelled. "We're all waiting for you."

I walked slowly back to my bedroom and watched from my window as Greg and Kenny climbed into the backseat of the car.

This is crazy, I thought. I had no intention of going with them to the airport. I was going ice skating with Jerry and his cousin who was visiting from Connecticut. That would certainly be more fun than seeing Greg off. Then why, I wondered, had the lump in my throat come back?

I hadn't seen much of my girl friends during Christmas vacation, not even M. J. I didn't speak to her very much on the phone, either. A couple of times she called when I was on my way out, and once I cut our conversation short because I was waiting for a call from a boy I had a date with that night. After that, M. J. didn't initiate any calls, but at the time I was too preoccupied to notice.

I made a special point of meeting my friends at Rico's the first Friday after the holiday. I was the last to arrive because Carl had insisted that I look at a new character he had created for his Walnuts strip. Carl explained that the fluffy-haired creature he had drawn was going to be Walnuts' girl friend.

"She's cute, but a little wimpish."

"That's what I was afraid of. You've really got a good eye, Amy."

"Call me tonight, and we'll talk about it. I've really got to go now."

We had been standing on the school steps, and I hurried off. I smiled to myself all the way to Rico's, thinking that Carl, the loner, was obviously smitten with me. It was a miracle that he not only asked my opinion, but accepted my criticism.

My friends were sitting in our usual booth at Rico's and I slid in next to M. J. No one greeted me, but Gail was bubbling on about the ski trip she'd had in Vermont.

"The skiing was superb, and the best part was jumping into a Finnish bath afterwards. Can you imagine getting out of a swimming pool in below-freezing weather, surrounded by snow? It was crazy!"

The girls laughed appreciatively and Gail said, "I haven't stopped talking. Now tell me the highlights of your vacation." Her eyes shifted to Terry and M. J., and didn't include me.

Terry mentioned a new man she'd met — a freshman at Penn — who'd invited her to a spring weekend house party. "He's the son

108

of my father's college roommate, which is the only reason my parents are letting me go. I don't know why parents believe that you can't get into trouble if you don't leave home."

"Let's not tell them," M. J. said, smiling.

"What's new with you and Bud?" Gail asked.

"We're tighter than ever. And I'm planning to give him a Mexican party for his birthday. We'll have tacos, and enchiladas, and sangria, and instead of party hats, everyone will have to wear a sombrero."

"Terrific idea. We'll help you, right, Terry?" Gail said.

"Of course," Terry agreed.

Again, I felt excluded, and I wanted to get into the conversation. "I'm almost glad the vacation is over so I can get some rest." I was trying to be funny, but nobody laughed.

"The price of being too popular," Terry said.

I could feel my cheeks getting pink, because I hadn't meant to sound like I was bragging. M. J., almost as a reflex action, helped me out by diverting everyone's attention.

"Gail, I really like your hair like that." Gail was no longer wearing a braid, and her hair had been cut to shoulder length.

"Thanks," Gail said. "I got tired of my pig tail, which I've had since fourth grade."

"It's glamorous," Terry remarked. "Makes you look older."

"It does look good," I said.

"Surprised you noticed." Gail narrowed her eyes at me, and I had to look away.

There was no mistaking her hostility, but there wasn't much I could say without getting into a hassle. I was glad when the others decided it was time to leave.

It had started to rain, and there was a chill in the air as we made our way to the corner. The weather put a damper on our conversation, which suited me fine since no one was talking to me anyway. Then Terry and Gail took off in different directions, which forced me and M. J. to be alone. I was tempted to ask if Gail and Terry were mad at me, but I already knew the answer. They obviously were. For that matter, M. J. didn't seem overly friendly, either.

We walked along in silence, and when we reached my house, I just had to say something. "What's the matter with everyone today? Nobody spoke to me."

"I guess they don't think you're interested in them."

"You know that isn't true," I murmured. "It's just that I'm trying to recover from Jeff."

"And in the process you're neglecting all your old friends."

"That's not true," I said, without conviction.

"Even me," she added softly.

There was a real downpour then, and we both must have looked like waifs standing there, soaked to the skin, our hair like two wet mops. It would have been comical if I hadn't thought that it wasn't just raindrops that were rolling down M. J.'s face, but tears as well.

M. J. mumbled good-bye and ran off, while I turned to go into my house. Probably it was my imagination that she was actually crying. Besides, I had to hurry and blow-dry my hair before I got picked up that evening. I didn't want to go out with my hair resembling a ball of frizz.

Thirteen

In the beginning of March I began getting invitations to the Senior Prom. Every boy I went out with eventually asked if he could escort me, and I found myself with more invitations than I could handle. Not that I didn't enjoy my position of being able to pick and choose, but there really wasn't a single boy I particularly wanted to go with. I had to think of ingenious methods of putting each one who invited me on "hold" until I made up my mind. My best way of not saying yes was a vague, "That's really nice of you to ask me." That was neither a negative response or a firm commitment, and left the door open until I made a decision. I even considered going alone, believing I would dance every dance, and possibly be the belle of the ball.

By the first of April, I'd already received half a dozen bids. I made a list and wrote a brief description of each boy. This was my twentieth-century version of what was called in the olden days a "Chap Book." Mumsie showed me one that belonged to her mother — my great grandmother. It was a leather-bound book, each page decorated with pastel-colored hearts and flowers, and descriptions of chaps to match. They were "handsome, witty, and rich," or "elegant, debonair, graceful." Apparently my great grandmother could only see the good side of her chaps.

I was much less generous in my evaluations, and the negatives outweighed the positives by far. When I studied the results, which was a little like reviewing a horse's previous performance before making a bet, I was still in a quandary. It was possible for me to predict what the prom would be like with each entry. I could just hear David spending the evening giving me an analysis of the band: "You call that music?"; Carl criticizing the decor: "Whoever dreamt up that color combination must have been color blind. Purple and green don't work!"; Jerry unable to hide his conceit: "The ambience would have been improved if I'd worked on the committee."; Alan wailing in computerese: "There's a new user-friendly software program that integrates the world!"; Preston, preening, and probably saying nothing. And on and on, with every other candidate.

The closer it came to Senior Prom time, the more uncertain I became about whose invitation I should accept. In a perverse way,

I was in the same position I was a year ago. Then, at least, I had a support system from my friends and my family. Now I was on my own. It didn't make sense that I was better off needing an escort, than not knowing which one I should choose. I desperately needed to talk to someone, but I didn't know who. I seemed to have alienated the world!

The distance between me and M. J. had widened, and Terry and Gail remained indifferent. When Greg came home for Easter vacation, he treated me like a polite stranger. In desperation, I might have turned to Kenny, who had always been my staunch supporter, but he had had it with me, too. Almost without me knowing it was happening, I had rejected him — and all because of a basketball shot!

We had a hoop over the garage door, and in good weather he could always persuade me to shoot some baskets with him. But the last three times he'd asked me, I was getting ready to go out. That meant I was pressing a blouse, or fixing my hair, or taking a bubble bath. Playing with my kid brother definitely did not fit into my schedule. I didn't think it was such a big deal that I'd been unavailable, but he didn't see it that way.

It was late Saturday afternoon, and I'd been messing around with some new makeup. Preston was taking me to a French restaurant in West Orange, and I decided to look as sophisticated as possible for the occasion. I'd just finished putting on my face when

Kenny pounded on my door, and then burst into my room.

"Doesn't do much good to knock if you don't wait for an answer."

"Sorry, Amy, but I'm too excited! I've got to show you."

"Show me what?" I asked.

"My hook shot. I can finally do it!"

"Not now, Kenny. Can't you see I'm getting ready to go out?"

"That's what you said the last time, and the time before that, and the time —"

"Well, I'm not lying."

"No, you're not, and you're also not fun anymore!" He stormed out of my room and slammed the door.

"Kenny. . . ." I ran to open the door and call him back and explain that it was nothing personal and that. . . . But it was too late. He was already out of sight, probably practicing his hook shot by himself, without me to admire him.

A couple of days later I tried to make it up to him. There was about a half hour before my parents would be home and we were on kitchen duty. I was fixing the salad and Kenny was setting the table. He was whistling to himself, which was one way of not talking. He was still mad that I hadn't taken the time to let him show off for me, but I was sure I could change all that.

"Hey, Kenny," I said, as though I'd been waiting all my life for this moment, "now is the time!"

He had just folded the last napkin beside a plate, and stopped whistling long enough to ask, "Time for what?"

"For you to show me your hook."

"You don't really care." He was scowling at me.

"I do, or I wouldn't be asking." I flashed him a smile, hoping I could win him over.

"You know something, Amy, I don't believe you." With that, he did a disappearing act and left me standing there.

"You're acting like a two-year-old," I muttered under my breath. Of course he couldn't hear me, but I had to say something that would make me feel better, even if I didn't believe it myself.

It was less than three days later that I got into a real hassle with my mother. Usually we got along great, and her way of showing disapproval was to tell me that she didn't think something was a good idea. That was the only admonition I needed to make me shape up. But this time my behavior triggered a reaction that I was totally unprepared for. Thinking about it later, it was probably a result of me not taking time to talk to my mother for several months. Since she knew how unhappy I was about Jeff, she probably didn't want to add to my problems by laying guilt on me about not communicating with her. I guess there was bound to be an explosion.

It was the second Saturday in April, and

I had slept late. When I woke up I saw a large note Scotch-taped across my mirror telling me to come immediately to Evelyn's house. Evelyn was my mother's best friend. She lived around the corner and didn't have any children. She and her husband owned a local ad agency, and they treated me like their own daughter. Evelyn was a writer, so we had a lot in common, besides the fact that she was a lot of fun and I really liked her.

The note was brief and to the point:

> Amy, please come to Evelyn's as soon as possible. Her mother has just passed away and Daddy and I will be there all afternoon. Evelyn wants to see you.
>
> Love, Mother

I was sorry to hear the news, but it wasn't totally unexpected. Evelyn's mother had suffered a heart attack and been in the intensive care unit of the local hospital for ten days. I'd heard my mother saying just two days before that Evelyn didn't expect her mother to recover. It was very sad, and I knew that Evelyn would be undone, but I was sure my mother had forgotten my plans for the day.

Charlie had invited me to go to the Meadowlands sports arena to see Bruce Springsteen in concert. The tickets were as scarce as a snowball in summer, and I was sure my mother wouldn't want me to miss it. It was after eleven, and the concert was scheduled for two o'clock. Charlie was picking me up at twelve-thirty so there was no way I could make it to Evelyn's and back in time. I could visit her the next day, or the day after, but when would I have another opportunity to see Bruce in person?

I scribbled a note to my mother and left it on the hall table.

Dear Mom,

Sorry to hear about Evelyn's mother. I will try and get over there tomorrow. You probably forgot I was going to the Meadowlands today to hear Bruce Springsteen. If it were anything else, I would have canceled the date. Be sure and send Evelyn my love.

Amy

I honestly didn't think any more about Evelyn because I was concerned about what I would talk to Charlie about all the way to the concert. Conversation with him was a strain, because he was either tongue-tied or droned on about his favorite subject, chess. But I knew the concert would be sensational, even if my date was less than scintillating.

One good thing about Charlie was that he was too shy, even after a half-dozen dates, to hold my hand. As I put on my electric blue blouse and white wool skirt — my outfit that I wore only on special occasions — I thought, What a waste on Charlie. He wouldn't notice if I came dressed in a paper bag!

The last time I'd worn that combination was with Jerry to go disco dancing. Jerry kept telling me how great I looked, how I should always wear that shade of blue, and that I should consider becoming a fashion writer. Naturally, I was flattered, but after a while I began to question his sincerity. Especially because when he wasn't saying something dripping with syrup, he was talking about himself. And he should have known that I wanted to be a serious novelist. I'd told him enough times, but it must not have sunk in.

Also, unlike Charlie, Jerry seemed to believe that the number of kisses we had was directly related to the number of times we'd gone out together. On my last date with Jerry, I kidded him about my theory as we stood outside my door. I managed to extricate myself from his embrace and asked him point blank:

"If we go out twenty times, does that mean you're entitled to twenty kisses?"

"Don't be ridiculous, Amy. It's just that I like you. Actually, you're the first girl I've been interested in on a serious basis."

"I'm flattered, Jerry, but I'm not ready for that kind of relationship."

"At least you're honest. I must know, though, if there's anyone else."

"No, there's no one." That was truer than ever, now that Jeff had found someone new.

"Then you'll still go out with me?"

"Of course. But you have to forget about the 'kiss for every date' policy."

"I'll try," he said, smiling. Then he added, lest I forget how wonderful he was, "Lucky for you I'm so agreeable — without being a wimp — and have such a good sense of humor besides."

At least with Charlie, I thought, as I gave myself a final appraisal in front of the full-length mirror inside my closet door, I won't get into a wrestling match. And I won't feel crowded all evening by an ego as big as a house.

The concert lived up to my expectations, and afterwards we went to the Peppermint Corner, which specializes in oversized sandwiches and giant ice-cream sodas. It was a perfect evening in every way, except for the fact that our conversation slowly ground to a halt after ten minutes. I had to keep reminding myself how sweet Charlie was, but I wasn't unhappy when he suggested we go home. It was only ten o'clock, an embarrassingly early hour to end a Saturday night, but it didn't bother Charlie at all.

I thanked him profusely for taking me to the concert. Then he shook my hand vigorously, and we said good-night. "I'll call you, Amy," he said, and ran off.

"I know," I murmured, almost resignedly, and went into the house.

I wasn't surprised to see my parents were still up. I hung my coat in the hall closet and strolled into the den where they were watching tv. Neither of them bothered to look up, but I figured they must be involved in a really good program.

"Hi," I greeted them, standing at the threshold of the door.

Some indistinguishable sound came out of my mother, and my father barely nodded his head.

It didn't take two seconds for me to realize something was terribly wrong. Usually — although not in recent months, come to think about it — my father welcomed me as though I'd just returned from a long trip when he hadn't seen me for a few hours. And when I was dressed up, he invariably paid me some exaggerated compliment like, "I don't see what's so great about Brooke Shields," or, "If all else fails, you can always be a movie star." His flattery was so bizarre I always had a fit of the giggles. But lately . . . nothing.

I sat down on a straight-backed chair that faced the television set and tried to blend into the scene. They were watching a popular sit-com and I could tell by the studio audience reaction that something very funny had just transpired. I looked at my parents, but neither of them cracked a smile.

When the commercial came on, my father stood up and turned to my mother. "I guess I'm not in the mood for this, dear. Think I'll go to bed and do some reading."

He swept past me without even a glance, and I felt as if I'd been brushed by a glacial wind. It was true that my father hadn't talked to me much lately, but he'd never treated me like a nonperson!

"What's wrong with Daddy?" I asked.

"You don't have any idea?" My mother looked grim.

"I guess I must have done something." It was lucky I was sitting down because I suddenly felt very weak.

"It's more what you haven't done, Amy."

"I don't know what you mean."

"Neither your father nor I can believe that going to a rock concert had priority over dropping in on Evelyn. You didn't even have the courtesy to call! Evelyn asked about you at least half a dozen times, and Daddy and I exhausted all possible excuses. When I finally called home, and there was no answer, I was sure you were on the way over. Fortunately, she had a lot of visitors, but the last thing Evelyn said before we left was, 'I hope Amy is okay. Be sure and send her my love.'"

"I didn't know it would mean so much to her to see me," I said lamely.

"That's a convenient excuse, and unacceptable." I'd never seen my mother so angry, and I tried to keep myself from crying.

"I'll go tomorrow. I promise."

"That doesn't make up for you not appearing today."

"Then what will make up for it?" My voice was trembling.

"I'm not sure anymore. For the past few months I've been put in the position of protecting you. I knew you were going through a difficult period, and I tried to justify your behavior to your father, and to Greg, and just last week to Kenny. But now I have to admit they have a point."

"Well, they just don't understand. Kenny's too young, and Daddy and Greg probably never had an unhappy love affair."

"You're the first person in the world to have this experience. Is that what you think?"

"Yes, that's what I think," I answered, my defenses crumbling. And I fled to my room before I was totally dissolved in tears.

*F*ourteen

For the next few days the merry-go-round I was on seemed to go faster and faster, and it took everything I had to hang on. I glided through the daily routine on egg shells, trying not to let my family's attitude get to me. They didn't exactly give me the silent treatment, but everything was different. The one area of my life that hadn't changed, and still sustained me, was being popular with boys.

Also, I kept up my school work. Academic grades were crucial and I didn't want to blow my chances of getting into the college of my choice. So no matter how preoccupied I was with boys, I always found time to do my homework, get my papers in on time, and cram for exams. Except for the *Swen*, and the volleyball team, I spent all my free time preparing for the weekends.

The last thing in the world I wanted to do was take on any outside activities. But I

124

couldn't say no to Ms. Kelly, our gym teacher, when she asked me to supervise the seventh-grade volleyball match on Teaneck's Junior High Field Day.

In tenth grade I had been captain of the volleyball team, and since that time I'd always been a pet of Ms. Kelly's. Ms. Kelly was an apple-cheeked, gray-haired lady, who constantly blasted away on her permanently attached whistle to show how tough she was. But actually she was a pussycat, and all the girls loved her. It was considered a privilege to be offered any special responsibility by her. Therefore, even though Junior High's Field Day was scheduled for the third Saturday in April — the day I had saved to go shopping for a prom dress — I assured her I'd be there.

"Remember," she warned me, "the volleyball game is scheduled for twelve noon, but to be on the safe side you'd better be there at least fifteen minutes early."

"Don't worry," I said. "I'll be on time."

The night before Field Day I set my alarm for eight-thirty, an unprecedented hour to get up on a Saturday. But I had to hit the stores as soon as they opened or I wouldn't be able to cover all of them. I'd put off doing even a little preliminary research for a dress because I hadn't had time, and also because I hadn't yet decided whose invitation I would be accepting. However, Senior Prom time was getting close, and I knew if I actually splurged on a dress, I would be forced to make a decision.

I couldn't delay any longer, and I had no excuses. I even had the money. Every Christmas, in addition to an elaborate gift, Mumsie gave me some money that she insisted I spend on something special to wear. Fortunately, I had saved most of it, and I knew if I wasn't too extravagant I might have some left over for shoes.

The stores didn't open until nine-thirty, but by the time I dragged myself out of bed, got dressed, and mapped out which ones I would cover, I didn't even have time for coffee. On my way out, I popped my head in the kitchen where everyone was having a civilized breakfast and explained where I was going.

"Can't you have a piece of toast?" my mother asked.

"No time. Got to help out at Field Day."

Before she could protest, I ducked out. But then I distinctly heard my father say, "Let her go."

I wasn't sure how to interpret that. Did it mean he was defending me, or that he didn't care if I starved? Lately, my humor had become uncharacteristically black.

It was a delicious spring day, and I thought how happy I should be that I could afford to go shopping, had been "picked" by a favorite teacher to officiate at a volleyball match, had a zillion invites to the Senior Prom, and a calendar filled solid for a month. Lucky me,

I thought, as I trotted toward the mall, where there were a string of boutiques with delectable offerings.

Then why, I wondered, do I feel so peculiar? Something was definitely out of sync. I tried to attribute my weird feelings to the fact that I hadn't had any breakfast, but I knew that wasn't true. The hollowness in the pit of my stomach had nothing to do with lack of food. I was hungry for friendship, and this solitary shopping expedition made me painfully aware of my loneliness.

Ordinarily I would have gone shopping with M. J., or Gail, or Terry. Maybe all three. We'd case the stores, help one another make decisions, try not to giggle when we saw the salesperson was being quietly driven up the wall. Shopping with my friends was always hilarious . . . but now, now I was on my own and there was no way it could be any fun. It didn't make me feel any better when I recalled that just a couple of weeks ago they were talking about their prom dresses that they'd bought together one Saturday. I couldn't have gone with them even if they'd asked me . . . but they hadn't.

"Well, Amy Ross," I said, biting my lip, "you're really on your own. And you might as well buy the most smashing gown you can find. Something that will have every boy at the prom gasping!"

With that in mind, I marched into the first boutique on my list, The Purple Onion. A sleepy-eyed young woman, wearing a large name pin that read "Lois," was perched on a stool, her arms stretched out on a jewelry counter.

"Anything special you want?" she asked in an indifferent manner.

"I'm looking for a prom dress," I told her.

"Over there." She pointed to a row of dresses lined against the wall. "What color and size?"

"Anything but lavender. I had that last year. And I'm a size five or six."

"There are still a few things left. Help yourself. You can try them on in the fitting room," she said, pointing to the far corner of the room. "And you can see how they look in the three-way mirror." She tilted her head toward the large mirror in the center of the store.

"Thanks," I said, and proceeded to whisk through the rack. I pulled out several gowns — a poison green with floppy short sleeves, a taxi-cab yellow with a dramatically low back, and a plain, pale blue strapless.

Each time I came out to view myself in the mirror, Lois swiveled around on her stool and said, "That's nice."

I thought how much fun it would have been if M. J. and Gail and Terry had been there to see Lois's laid-back manner. She seemed as if she didn't care about making a sale. I figured she must be a relative of the owner's, or she never would have the job. But there was no one I could share this information with. I tried not to think about that, and continued trying things on.

"The yellow is a possibility, but I'm not sure. I'll be back later if I change my mind."

"No problem," Lois said, as I put all the gowns back in place.

My next stop was a few doors down called Out of Sight. This was a fancier boutique that took up two floors, and I was directed up a winding staircase to a department called "Prom Corner." A zippy woman waited on me and showed me half a dozen possibilities. She oohhed and aahhed about each one and I knew I couldn't trust her opinion. But one lipstick red dress with spaghetti straps really grabbed me.

"Can you put this aside for me?" I asked.

"I can put it on hold until noon. Will you let me know by then?"

"Promise," I said, gave her my name, and rushed out.

I knew I wouldn't be satisfied if I didn't check out the other shops on my list, in addition to the Young Sophisticate floor in the department store. I hurried through the other boutiques and finally narrowed my choices to a blue-and-white dotted swiss with a low neck and puffed sleeves, and the red. Did I want the demure or the siren look? If only I had a friend to advise me! I felt more alone than ever.

I bought an ice-cream cone and sat down on a bench to mull over my problem. Although I'd established my independence, I couldn't help wondering what each boy's preference would be. Charlie wouldn't notice, Preston would be too concerned about his own physical image to care about mine, and the others. . . . It didn't really matter.

I finally decided to take a risk and go with the red. If I wanted to play the role of femme fatale, I might as well look the part. I went back to Out of Sight, and had to wait while my salesperson convinced a chubby young teenager who was on the verge of tears that she did not look like a pink balloon in the dress she was trying on. I overheard the girl's disapproving mother say, "Maybe now, Lucille, you'll cut out desserts."

By the time I paid for my dress, and had it wrapped up, it was eleven-thirty. As she handed me my package, my salesperson couldn't stop her pitch: "You're going to look divine at the prom, but you must have shoes to match the red."

"You're right," I said, thinking that was the first honest piece of advice she'd given me.

I knew it was cutting it close, but I figured I'd have time to pop into Shoetown, which was on my way home, and buy some sandals. It made sense, because I had the dress with me and I could get an exact match. However, I didn't count on having a young man wait on me who was obviously new, didn't know the stock, brought out the wrong size, and couldn't distinguish red from purple. He told me his name was Joe, he only worked Saturdays, and he was going to college. The last thing I wanted to hear was his life story, and I told him I was in a terrible hurry. That didn't seem to make much of an impression, and the whole process took twice as long as it should have. I was at the point of no return. I began to panic when I knew I'd never make it to Field Day by quarter to twelve. I was about to leave when Joe brought me the perfect red sandals, the right size, with a high, narrow heel.

I had just enough money to pay for them, and then I streaked out of there. There was no time for me to stop at my house so I bolted toward school at breakneck speed, clutching my bundles. I was panting for breath, and beads of perspiration were pouring down my face when I arrived at the volleyball court.

I could see immediately what had happened and my heart sank. Ms. Kelly had recruited Molly, a blond string bean who was captain of the tenth-grade volleyball team, to take my place.

"Uh-oh," I muttered, feeling a pang of jealousy. "I can see I have been replaced."

I saw Ms. Kelly about fifty feet away supervising a relay race. A group of parents were wildly cheering their kids on, and I wandered over to watch from the sidelines until the race was finished. I wasn't sure what I could say to Ms. Kelly, but I hoped by some miracle I'd find the right words.

She was chatting with parents when the

race was over. As soon as she caught my eye she excused herself and walked over to where I was standing.

"I'm really sorry," I began. "I lost track of time and I was sure I'd make it by twelve, at the latest, but it took me ten times longer than —"

"Never mind excuses, Amy. Fortunately, although I waited until the last minute, I found someone to take over."

"But you don't understand. . . ."

"Oh, yes, I do. I see you haven't been struck down by the bubonic plague or hit by a truck. The only reasonable explanation." There was a hard glint in her eye that told me she wasn't being funny. "It seems to me," she added coldly, glancing at my packages, "that Field Day interrupted your shopping."

"It was my only chance to get something for the prom, and I had to find shoes to match my dress. . . ." I practically choked on the words, they sounded so insignificant.

"Forget it, Amy. I was counting on you, and you let me down."

"Ms. Kelly, please . . . I didn't mean to. . . ."

But she had already stalked off, and a bunch of little kids had surrounded her, clamoring for attention.

I stood there for a moment watching, feeling like a stranded calf. I wasn't needed anymore, and there was nothing for me to do but go home.

Fifteen

I walked home slowly, still dazed by Ms. Kelly's reaction. But I couldn't blame her and I was filled with self-reproach. If only I hadn't bothered about the shoes. I could have found time to look for them before the prom . . . after school one day, or Thursday night when the stores stayed open late. My mother would have taken me. . . . A pair of sandals wasn't worth destroying Ms. Kelly's faith in me.

There was no one home, which was just as well, because I wasn't up to explaining why I'd returned from Field Day so early. Just another incident that would justify my parents being annoyed with me.

I trudged into my room, unwrapped my purchases, and stuck them in the closet. Normally, I would have tried the whole outfit on, but I wasn't in the mood. I had a whole afternoon to kill, and nothing to do. It was much too early to think about getting ready to go out that night. I didn't particularly feel like reading. Even though it was a perfect day for a sun tan, I didn't feel like lying alone on a lounge chair in our backyard.

Maybe it was a form of punishment, but I decided to stay indoors and attack my homework. I sat down at my desk, and it was then I noticed a letter next to my typewriter. I could see from the thickness of the envelope that it was a college bulletin. I'd already received several, but this was the one I'd been waiting for. It was from Sanders, a small college in New England, famous for its excellent literature and writing program. My heart beat faster as I opened the envelope, pulled out the material, and read the form letter:

Dear High School Junior:

Thank you for your interest in our college. Enclosed you will find a questionnaire that we use to determine the interests and needs of high school students who are considering attending Sanders College in the future. We retain the information we receive from your response and will take it into consideration should you decide to apply to our institution.

We would like to stress that we place great emphasis on the essay question, number 5.

We look forward to hearing from you before May 15.

                    Sincerely,

                    Alice P. Hubbard
                    Dean of Admissions

I skimmed the first four questions, all standard queries about what schools I'd attended, summer job experience, extracurricular activities, major interests. Then I turned to question 5, pleased that the essay question carried so much weight. After all, writing was my strong point!

The question read: Write a brief autobiography that includes the values that are important in your life.

That's easy, I thought, as I rolled a clean sheet of paper into my typewriter. I can pound something out this afternoon, and get it in the mail this evening.

I started out like gangbusters, describing my role as the middle child, and only girl, in the family; the advantages of living in a suburban community close to New York; the security of having gone to the same school all my life.

This was only a rough draft, and my fingers flew over the keyboard as I wrote whatever came into my head. I filled a whole page, read what I had written, and realized I hadn't yet mentioned anything that had to do with values.

Values, I murmured, values. I put a fresh sheet in the typewriter, poised my hands over the keys — but nothing happened. Both my mind and my fingers froze.

You know what values are, I told myself. Values are what's important and worthwhile. They're what give meaning to life. And what's important to me. . . . I couldn't bring myself to write what I knew to be the truth. For the past few months, the only thing of value in my life had been boys.

I pushed my chair back from my desk and started to get up. I felt very shaky and slightly dizzy, as though I'd received some shocking bad news. And in a way, that's exactly what had happened. Slowly, and insidiously, I had destroyed all the relationships that had meant anything to me. I had sacrificed my friends and my family in order to be popular with boys.

I made my way into the bathroom and splashed my face with cold water. I had a case of *déja vu* as I looked in the mirror and remembered the vow I'd made not to let my split with Jeff turn me into a wimp. I hadn't become a wimp, but something much worse — a selfish paper doll.

There was nothing wrong in thinking about the opposite sex and I didn't know a single girl who didn't, but I had gone overboard. I had acquired a long string of boys, most of whom I really didn't care about. If I was really honest, I'd used them to feed my ego.

I dried my face, returned to my room, and collapsed on my bed. I was overcome with a sense of shame as I relived the pattern of my inconsiderate behavior. My family and my friends had all dropped hints about how I had changed, but I had conveniently ignored them. My father's remark that I was a boarder in the house; Greg half kiddingly stopping me on the way out one day to introduce himself; Kenny telling me I was no fun anymore; M. J. coming right out and saying I was neglecting my old friends; Evelyn's surprise at my indifference to her; Ms. Kelly's disappointment. . . .

I don't know how long I lay there immobilized — an hour, maybe two. I must have been in a kind of stupor because I didn't hear anyone come into the house. Then suddenly I felt a hand on my shoulder. I turned and saw my mother standing over me, a look of concern on her face.

"Are you okay, Amy?" she asked, gently.

"I'm not okay. I'm awful," I murmured.

My mother looked very worried and put her hand on my forehead. "Are you sick? Does anything hurt?"

"Everything," I answered, pulling myself up to a sitting position. My body trembled and the tears streamed down my face.

My mother sat down beside me on the bed and instinctively put her arms around me. She didn't say anything for the longest time, and I clung to her like a little kid until my weeping subsided.

"Need a hanky," I mumbled, reverting to that childish word for handkerchief that I hadn't used in years.

My mother reached for the box of Kleenex that was on my night table and handed me several tissues. I blew my nose and blotted my eyes.

"Did something happen to you?" my mother asked finally. "Something at Field Day?"

"That's only part of it. Something's been happening to me for months and I. . . ." I started blubbering again.

"You've been going through a rough time, Amy. We all wanted to help you, but you couldn't see it that way. Even though some of us weren't too subtle. . . ." She half smiled at me.

"Everyone's mad at me," I sniffled. "I'm not just talking about you and Daddy and Greg and Kenny. It's everyone else, too."

"You seem to get plenty of phone calls." My mother was trying to cheer me up.

"Yes, but from all the wrong people. I hardly ever hear from M. J. anymore . . . or Gail . . . or Terry. I've been so determined to be popular with boys I don't even care about, that I've lost all my real friends. They seem to have deserted me, but I can't say that I blame them."

"If you can admit that, you've come a very long way, Amy."

"I can admit it, but what good will it do me?"

"I think you should call M. J. and tell her exactly what you've told me. See what happens."

"What if she doesn't want to listen, or has a new best friend, or. . . ."

"You won't be any worse off than you are now."

"You're right about that, Mom. I guess I need a lot of forgiving from a lot of people . . . starting with you and Daddy."

"We've always been proud of you, Amy, but after today I think we'll be prouder than ever. It takes more courage to admit you're wrong than to make excuses."

"Lately, that's all I've been doing. It's been kind of exhausting." For the first time all day, I managed to smile.

"You can't undo overnight what's been building up for so long, but you're halfway there once you recognize the problem."

"You really believe that?"

"I know it for sure, Amy." My mother stood up, and headed for the door. She turned, just before she left the room, and said, "Remember, all it takes is courage."

I suddenly felt a lot better, having unburdened myself and knowing my mother still loved me. It's funny, I mused, this morning my main problem had been finding a dress and shoes for the Senior Prom, and trying to decide whose invitation I should accept. And now, none of that seemed the least bit important.

I was still feeling a little shaky, but I

forced myself to get up. I wandered over to my typewriter, where the blank piece of paper was staring me in the face. It didn't look so threatening anymore, and I thought, Now I can finish my essay easily. I no longer have to be ashamed of my values.

It was five o'clock and I had a couple of hours before I was being picked up. Plenty of time to call M. J. I determinedly strode into the hall, brought the phone into my room, closed my door, sat down on the floor, and leaned my back against my bed. My usual position for telephone conversations.

I picked up the receiver and was about to dial, but I was overcome with panic. What would I say? What if M. J. didn't want to talk to me? What if she hung up? An insistent buzzing reminded me that I had the receiver off the hook, and I replaced it. Then I stared at the phone as though it were some alien force. I reminded myself of what my mother had said about calling M. J.: "You won't be any worse off than you are now," and, "All it takes is courage."

"Courage," I whispered, took several deep breaths, and although I had trouble controlling my trembling hand, I managed to dial the correct number.

There were two rings, and I half hoped no one would answer. Then I wouldn't even have to leave a message. After a third ring, however, someone picked up. It was M. J. She was home. I had no excuses.

"It's me, Amy," I began, after she said hello. I tried to sound normal.

"Amy. . . ," she repeated, obviously surprised. "Amy. . . ."

"Yes, it's me."

"Are you all right?"

"I am and I'm not," I said idiotically.

"What part of you is which?"

"At least you're speaking to me, so that part's better."

"Amy, you're not making too much sense."

"I know I'm not, M. J., and I haven't for ages, but it wasn't until I got this questionnaire about values that everything came to a head and I realized . . . I realized what I'd become and how much I missed you."

My voice trailed off, and my eyes filled with tears. I clutched the phone, waiting for M. J. to say something. What if she didn't believe me, or worse, didn't care? It seemed to take forever, but finally she spoke.

"I've missed you, too," she said, softly.

"You have? You're not mad at me?" I held my breath, afraid of what she might say.

"Unhappy about you, hurt, I guess, but not really mad."

"And you tried to warn me, but I was too wrapped up in myself to pay attention."

"You were busy every minute."

"I know, and I never felt so lonely in my life. Today was the worst. . . . I've just got to talk to you."

"We both have to make up for lost time. There's lots I have to tell you, too."

"About you and Bud?" I asked.

"Mainly. I really need to see you." That was the most reassuring thing she could have said.

"And me you. How about tomorrow?"

"You mean you don't have a date?" I knew she was teasing me, but I answered seriously, "Nothing's more important than seeing you, M. J."

"I was going bike-riding with Gail and Terry, but we can all go together."

"Uh-oh," I sighed. "I don't think that's such a good idea. I'm not sure they'll want me along."

"Look, Amy, I can't say that they haven't felt . . . bad about you, but even Gail said the other day that Fridays at Rico's weren't what they used to be. What she meant was, we all missed you."

"If I could only believe that. . . ." My voice trembled and I was on the verge of tears again.

"I know it will be okay. I'll call them tonight and tell them how you feel. It may not happen right away, but I know they'll come around."

"If only that could happen. . . ."

"We'll make it happen. Don't worry. Meanwhile, why don't you come over tomorrow about ten so we can talk before anyone else shows up."

"That's the best invitation I've had in months. And M. J., you are what friendship is all about!"

Sixteen

I rode my bike to M. J.'s, parked it in the driveway, and hurried to the kitchen door. M. J.'s mother must have been watching me from the window, because she opened the door even before I got a chance to knock. I was a little surprised, and pleased, when she threw her arms around me. It wasn't like Mrs. Gibson to be demonstrative, but she seemed genuinely happy to see me.

"M. J.'s upstairs," she said. I was glad that she didn't make some remark about not seeing me for such a long time.

"I guess I'm early. I'll surprise her."

I bounded up the stairs. The door to M. J.'s room was open and she was sitting on her unmade bed, lacing up her sneakers. I stood at the threshold, not knowing what to say.

"Amy, you're early," M. J. observed, glancing up at me.

"I know. Guess I was anxious." I smiled foolishly.

I think we were both kind of embarrassed, and trying to have an ordinary conversation.

"Well, why don't you come in and make yourself at home?" M. J. stood up, and made an elaborate gesture of welcome.

"Good idea." I stepped into the room, and probably because I was suffering an acute state of nerves, I tripped. I tried to break my fall by flinging out my arms, and succeeded in suspending my body in an arc, my hands on the bed, balancing the rest of me. It was such an absurd position that I started to giggle. A look of alarm had crossed M. J.'s face, but when she saw I wasn't hurt, she, too, broke out laughing. Then, with M. J.'s help, I managed to right myself. We were both dissolved in a fit of hilarity, laughing until the tears streamed down our faces. I knew it wasn't just my ridiculous entrance that caused our mini-hysteria, but a wonderful release from tension.

After that, it was just like it had always been between us. M. J. closed the door and we talked nonstop while I helped M. J. make her bed. We chatted about a lot of inconsequential things for a few minutes, but then M. J. became serious. I was sharply reminded how removed I'd been from what was going on in anybody's life but my own when M. J. confided that she and Bud were having their first major disagreement.

144

"Bud's been accepted at the University of Rochester, and he expects me to go there, too."

"Why wouldn't you?"

"Because I want to go to school out West next year, when I graduate. He's known that all along. He doesn't understand that it doesn't mean I want to break up with him. I just want a totally different environment."

"Would you each go out with other people?"

"That's part of it. My parents have always thought we were too young to be so tight, anyway. Besides, I have my senior year of high school coming up. Bud thinks if I go out with other guys next year, that'll be the end."

"Not if you mean as much to each other as you think."

"That's what I say. Anyhow, it's put an awful strain on our relationship. And you were the only person I wanted to talk to about it."

"I'm sorry, M. J. Sorry about everything."

"Where were you when I needed you the most?" She tried to smile.

"Probably having a miserable time with some guy I couldn't care less about. Anyhow, at least you and Bud are communicating. I know from experience, that's the most important thing." I sounded a little grim.

"You still like Jeff, don't you?"

"After going out with a zillion boys, I

know the answer to that one. . . . Yes."

"I guess I might soon be in the same boat with you."

"Or what might be described as the same shipwreck."

"At least you haven't lost your sense of humor, Amy."

Before I could answer, there was a banging on the door and then Gail's booming voice: "Are you two ever coming out? You're not the only one, M. J., who would like to get her hands on Amy."

"Uh-oh," I breathed, "she really sounds mad."

"You know Gail," M. J. whispered.

"That's why I'm scared," I said, only half kidding.

M. J. opened the door, and Gail was standing there, arms akimbo. "How did Miss America enjoy her tour away from the rest of the world?" she asked, her eyes boring into me.

"Come on, Gail. I'm here now." I wanted so much for everything to be all right.

"You don't know the effect you had on us," she growled.

"Yes, I do. . . . And I'm really sorry."

"There was a big hole at Rico's on Friday without you, Amy," Terry said, not unkindly.

"Yeah," Gail continued. "You were too occupied with being a debutante."

Gail wasn't making it easy for me, and besides, she was blocking the door.

"Hey, I thought we were going bike-riding." M. J. spoke up, pushed her way past Gail, and started down the stairs. Terry went next. Then Gail shrugged her shoulders, and followed, while I brought up the rear.

We released the brakes on our bikes, and started to straddle them, like a choreographed ballet. Then M. J. suggested we go to Gabriel's Park, about a mile away. "We can buy some hot dogs and sodas from the vendor. Something we haven't done in a long time."

"Sounds great," Terry said. "Okay with everyone else?"

"Fine with me," Gail agreed. "You know I love junk food. Does it suit you, Amy? You've been in such a rarefied atmosphere."

"Suits me," I answered, trying to ignore the obvious barb.

"Look, Gail," M. J. defended me, "Amy's back now."

"That's right, Gail. Give her a break," Terry said. I was grateful to her for taking my side. I even had a fleeting notion that now it was Gail who was being excluded, not me.

I guess it was that feeling that allowed me to say something really magnanimous. After all, if I could count on M. J. and Terry. . . .

"Gail, I'm not a debutante, I didn't like the rarefied atmosphere, and . . . and I missed the three of you more than you'll ever know."

"I believe that," M. J. said.

"Me, too," Terry chimed in.

There was a long silence, while Gail frowned and stared at me, as though she was coming to a hard decision. We all looked at her, waiting for a profound pronouncement. It was an odd scene, the four of us mounted on our bikes, waiting for Gail to say something that could change our relationships forever.

"Dummy," she said finally, her voice no longer angry, and a hint of a smile on her face, "that's what I've been trying to tell you. Without you . . . well, it just wasn't the same."

I wasn't sure whether I should laugh or cry, I was so relieved and happy. This was the closest Gail had ever come to being apologetic, and I think we were all a little surprised.

"Listen, you guys," Terry said, before we all sank into a sea of sentimentality, "enough of this! I, for one, didn't have breakfast, and I'm getting weak with hunger."

"I feel a little faint myself," I said.

M. J. gave me a slow wink, to let me know she knew what I meant. "Then before we all dissolve, let's get started," she said meaningfully, and began pedaling down the driveway.

I purposely waited until the others had fallen in line. I wanted to be the last, just in case I had an unexpected crying spell. I had to get used to everything that had happened. After all, it had been a painfully long time since I felt I had any friends.

We breezed along the road single file, and by the time we arrived at the park, I was euphoric. I felt once again that I belonged. The glorious spring day added to my sense of well-being.

The park was divided in such a way that one part was equipped with sandboxes and swings and see-saws for the little kids. The toddlers' squeals of delight mixed with the chatter of young parents. To me, it sounded like the sweetest music in the world, but then I was prepared to love everything. I had to chuckle when I heard Gail call to M. J., "Let's get away from all this noise!"

"Follow me," M. J. said, and led us to the other side of the park. Here there were places to sit and shade trees, and M. J. slowed to a halt. We all got off our bikes, and settled down at a couple of benches that were situated in front of a smoothed-off granite boulder that served as a table. Whoever designed the park had attempted to add a touch of rusticity to a suburban area. It didn't quite work, but I thought it was beautiful.

"Thank goodness he's here." Terry stood up and pointed to the hot dog vendor who was stationed with his cart under a tree about thirty feet away. "You guys want the usual — mustard and a Tab?"

We all nodded our heads, and Gail jumped up. "I'll help you," she volunteered. She probably wanted to say something privately about me to Terry, but I didn't care. It gave me a chance to talk to M. J.

"It was a little hairy for a minute with

Gail," I whispered, as soon as they took off.

"Yes, but it didn't take her long to come around."

"You paved the way," I said.

"Terry made it easy."

"Thanks to you, M. J., everything worked out."

"I told you it would." M. J. seemed just as happy as I was, and I was more grateful to her than ever.

Minutes later the girls returned with the food, which they carefully balanced on the boulder. Then we had a ridiculous conversation to determine how much each of us owed. I guess Terry and Gail had decided to lay off any further heavy discussion about me.

"Why don't we try dividing $6.47 by four, since that's what it cost?" Terry suggested.

"Not easy," Gail said.

"Pretend it was $7.00," I offered. "That makes it $1.75 each."

"Then I'm getting overpaid," Terry protested.

"Not if you subtract 14¼ cents," M. J. said.

"That makes it $1.61 and ¾ cents per person," Gail calculated, "and I'm not even good at math."

"I'll settle for $1.60," Terry said.

"*Bon appetit*," M. J. said, laughing, and we all settled down to some serious eating.

"Not exactly a gourmet meal," Gail remarked after she polished off her hot dog.

"Personally," I told her, recalling the boring times I'd had in fancy places, "I think this is better than any candlelit restaurant."

My three friends smiled at me, but didn't press for details. I think they all understood what I meant and that this was my way of telling them how overjoyed I was to be back.

After that, it was like one of our better sessions at Rico's. I was so totally accepted that my friends assumed I knew of some of the more recent developments in their lives. I listened carefully, so I didn't have to interrupt with a lot of questions, and remind them that I'd been out of it for so long, especially when the conversation turned to the Senior Prom.

"Have you decided who is the chosen one, Terry?" Gail asked.

"It's going to be Drew. He's a terrific dancer, and I don't have to get into a wrestling match on the way home. What about you?"

"I'm going with Doug," Gail answered.

"He's cute. Quiet, but very smart," I commented.

"Yes, he is that." Then Gail added good-naturedly, "And he's also the only boy who asked me."

We all laughed at Gail's honesty.

"And you?" Terry turned to me.

"Don't know yet. There's no one I really care about except. . . ."

"You can say it," Gail encouraged me.

She had been so forthright about herself, I thought it was silly of me to hold back. ". . . except Jeff," I finished.

"Have you spoken to him lately?" Terry asked.

"Not since . . . not for months. Come to think of it, I haven't seen him at school for a few days."

"Don't you know what happened to him last week?" M. J. looked shocked. "I was sure everybody knew."

"What happened?" I tried to keep my voice steady, but my heart was in my throat.

"Nothing that bad," Terry said quickly. She must have sensed how panicked I was.

"No, if you call breaking a leg not bad," Gail said. "Crashed into a tree when his bike swerved on a wet road."

"He broke a leg . . . and nobody told me. . . ." Then I added, "But why should anyone? We're not going together anymore."

"But you still like him," Terry observed, "so now's your chance, Amy."

"My chance for what?"

"He's still at home, and just as a friend, why don't you pay him a visit?"

"You've got to be kidding, Terry." The very thought of it had me breathing faster.

"I think that's not a bad idea," M. J. said. "Imagine if your roles were reversed. Wouldn't you be pleased if he came to see you if you were stuck in the house, nothing to do, probably suffering from cabin fever. . . ?"

"Well, yes, but then I like him and. . . ."

"You don't know that he doesn't still like you," Gail said with authority. "And there's only one way to find out."

"He's probably got a new girl friend. I saw him a couple of times with Sally Straus — a tenth-grader who's supposed to be a terrific chess player."

"You shouldn't have expected him to become a hermit, while you were living it up with a different guy every night." Gail sounded exasperated.

"No, but...."

"Give him a chance," Terry implored. "From my vast experience, I can tell you a boy with a broken leg is vulnerable and quite harmless. He's bound to be in a weakened condition and won't have the strength to throw you out of the house."

"That's right," M. J. agreed. "You can't be any worse off than you are now."

"You sound just like my mother. She said the exact same thing yesterday morning. And all this stuff about courage," I said.

"Was she right?" M. J. asked.

I looked at M. J., Gail, and Terry, and realized how courage had made our reconciliation possible.

"Hundred percent," I admitted.

"Then go for it," M. J. advised. "You know the importance of taking risks."

"I sure do," I said. "I've got absolutely nothing to lose."

Seventeen

I must have changed my mind a hundred times in the next ten minutes. It was one thing to philosophize about risk-taking, but quite another to put it into practice. It had worked once today with my girl friends, but I was superstitious about pressing my luck.

"Maybe I should write him a note," I said, "or send a get-well card. You know, something funny, showing I'm thinking about him but not . . . not unhinged or anything."

"That's chicken," Gail responded.

"But what if . . ." I continued.

"Forget the 'what ifs,' " M. J. interrupted.

" 'Cowards die many times before their deaths; the valiant never taste of death but once.' " Terry always had an appropriate Shakespearean quote.

"Never said I was valiant," I muttered.

"Just go see him," Gail urged. "If you procrastinate too long, he might be able to get up and run away."

"That's right," Terry said. "In fact, why don't you go now?"

"Now?" I repeated weakly.

"We'll escort you, if you want," M. J. said. "Sort of an armed guard."

"To make sure I get there or to catch me in case I'm thrown out of a window?" I laughed nervously.

"Your choice," M. J. said, trying to keep a straight face.

"I'll go by myself," I stated with unexpected resolve. "As you said, Gail, if I wait too long, he might get away."

Without another word, I unbraked my bike, mounted it, and started off.

"Good luck," my friends called to me in a chorus as I sped away.

I kept my eyes straight ahead, and waved my hand in the air to let them know I'd heard. I didn't dare look back for fear I'd lose my momentum, and change my mind.

All the way to Jeff's house, I tried out some opening lines:

Serious: "Hello, Jeff. Sorry to hear about your accident."

Funny: "What did you have against that poor innocent tree?"

Sarcastic: "You could have thought up a better way to get out of school."

Nothing seemed to strike the right tone,

and a block away from his house I was ready to call the whole thing off.

You can't back out now, my inner voice said.

"Why not? He'll never know."

You're already committed. Your friends will think you're gutless.

"They shouldn't have pressured me in the first place."

They knew you needed a push, and were doing you a favor.

"I don't have the slightest idea what to say to him."

You can wing it.

Then, as though I was being guided by remote control, I wheeled the rest of the way to Jeff's, leaned my bike against the side of his house, and rang the bell.

Jeff's mother came to the door, holding a tray of cookies. She was small and vivacious, and I was relieved to see that she seemed happy to see me. "Hello, Amy. Haven't seen you in a month of Sundays."

"Hi," I squeaked. "I've ... I — "

"Jeff's on the back porch. I was just about to bring him some cookies, but you can do it for me."

"Sure," I said, taking the tray, and wondering if I could ever speak again in anything but monosyllables.

I went through the living room, which led to the back porch, and saw Jeff before he saw me. His head was bent over a book, and his leg, in a cast up to his knee, was stretched out on a hassock. There was a portable radio and a pitcher of iced tea on a table next to him. Everything was within his reach, including a pair of crutches that were on the floor.

Trying to be casual, I swept into the room, placed the tray of cookies on the table, and sat down opposite him. His face registered such enormous surprise that I had to smile. Then he smiled, too, and mumbled, "You didn't have to come, Amy."

"You didn't have to go to such extremes to get us together," I joked. If I'd rehearsed that line, I never would have dared say it. At least I'd gotten my voice back, and Jeff was still smiling.

"How've you been?" he asked shyly.

"Okay. And you?"

"You can see how I am." He was just as uncomfortable as I was, which didn't make conversation easy.

"I mean, how are you otherwise?"

Jeff shrugged his shoulders, a form of body language that I interpreted as meaning he wasn't too great.

"Your mother told me to bring these cookies to you. I think she just made them."

"She's been baking a lot lately — ever since I've been confined. Help yourself."

I took a cookie, although I wasn't the least bit hungry. It would give me something to do.

"These are delicious," I said, taking a bite.

"My mother's a really good cook."

"I can tell."

Our conversation had never been so strained and inane, and I thought the best thing was for me to leave. I'd be doing us both a favor if I got out of there without causing further embarrassment to either of us. I would get up and make some polite remark about hoping he felt better soon. At least I'd tried.

Jeff must have sensed my imminent departure, because he said suddenly, "I think you'd like this." He held up the book he'd been reading.

"What is it?"

"Peter De Vries' latest novel. It's serious, but has all these puns that make it really funny."

"Like what?"

Jeff opened the book at random, glanced at a couple of pages, and quoted: "Tending a cemetery is a grave responsibility."

"That's good," I said, beginning to relax a little. "You know I'm a De Vries fan."

"How could I forget, Amy? That was one of the first things we had in common." I thought his face turned a little pink.

It had been so long since I'd talked about books to anyone! My favorite subject, but nobody cared about them the way Jeff did. The next thing I knew, Jeff was telling all the things he'd read in the past week.

"The only advantage to having a broken leg is that I've had plenty of time to read and to think."

"To think? What about?"

"Sort of reviewed in my mind this whole year. Do you know, it was just about a year ago that we . . . we started going together?"

"That's right. It began with the Junior Prom."

"That's when it started. And after that. . . ." He hesitated.

"After that, what?" I wanted him to go on reminiscing.

"After that, I had the best summer of my life." He smiled at me, that crooked smile that could always make me melt, and we looked deep into each other's eyes for the longest time.

"I have a confession," he said, almost abruptly.

"A confession? What have you done?" I asked in alarm.

"I haven't committed a crime exactly."

"But you've done something bad?"

"In a way, because I've wasted an awful lot of time."

"What do you mean?"

He took a deep breath, straightened up in his chair, looked me straight in the eye, and said, "I was wrong, and you were right, and I honestly think I've changed."

"Jeff, I'm not sure what you're talking about."

"Well, you told me all along that you had to do your own thing, be an individual . . . and I know now you were right."

"You mean you no longer think I was taking something away from us when I did things on my own?"

"That's exactly what I mean. In fact, I realize that one of the reasons I flipped for you was because you were independent. As you put it, we didn't have to be glued at the hip just because we were going together."

"Oh, Jeff," I exclaimed. "I'm . . . I'm so happy!"

"You see, one of the things I've learned recently is that I could never fall in love with a doormat."

"That's one thing I'm not," I assured him, and we both burst out laughing.

"Not that a doormat would do me much good, since I can't even walk now."

"How long will you be in a cast?" I asked.

"A few more weeks. I won't be going to the Senior Prom — not that I planned to."

"You didn't plan to? I thought for sure there was somebody you wanted to take."

"Not really." He had a knowing smile on his face, as though he knew exactly what I was thinking. "I haven't been interested in anyone."

"Not anyone?" I couldn't bring myself to come right out and ask him about Sally Straus.

"No one. Tried to keep busy, that's all."

"Me, too. I mean I didn't want to just sit home. And of course I'll go to the Senior Prom."

"Of course," he said. "I would expect you to."

I knew he wanted to know who I'd be going with, but was too shy to ask. Besides, I still didn't know the answer. Charlie, Alan, Jerry, Preston, David, Carl. . . .

Then it suddenly came to me, with a clarity I had never known in my life, who I would go with. It was Jeff. He was the one, always had been, always would be. I could barely contain my excitement, but I tried to be calm.

"You're going, too, Jeff."

"In a wheelbarrow?"

"No, on crutches."

"And who's going to hold me up?"

"You can lean on me. Look, I'll show you."

I got up, flipped on the portable radio to a music station, and handed him one of his crutches. He maneuvered himself out of his chair and stood up, balancing himself on one crutch. We stood facing each other, and he wrapped his free arm around my waist.

"I never was much of a dancer," he whispered in my ear.

"I know," I said, "and it never really mattered."

"Does this mean you'll go with me to the Senior Prom?"

"It's you or no one." That sounded like an exaggeration, but it was the absolute truth.

"Promise me you'll dance with other guys, even though you're with me?"

"Jeff, am I hearing right?"

"I told you I'd done a lot of thinking, Amy, and the one conclusion I've come to is that nothing terrible is going to happen if we're true to ourselves."

"I've done some thinking, too, lately. Believe it or not, I decided it's possible to have too much freedom." I thought of how I'd been a butterfly, unable to settle down, and not really enjoying flitting around from one boy to another.

"Amy, I think we should plant some flowers around that tree . . . that tree I crashed into."

"You mean the accident was worth it?"

"It was worth anything since it brought us together."

Then he pulled me to him and kissed me tenderly on the lips. When he finally let me go, I smiled up at him. "You mean even a broken leg?"

"You know it," he said, grinning impishly. And once again, only this time much more urgently, he pressed his lips against mine. For the first time in what seemed like a hundred long years, I felt I was the luckiest girl in the world.

Eighteen

Everything fell into place after that. As tactfully as possible I told the other boys who had invited me to the prom that I wouldn't be going with them. They all accepted the news with remarkable grace, especially when I said I was going with Jeff. Perhaps they knew that I'd never really gotten over him.

Then, almost magically, I no longer felt impelled to be busy every minute. The weekend before the prom, I actually canceled several dates. After dinner on Friday when we had finished the dishes, my father challenged me to a game of Scrabble. We hadn't ever had a confrontation, but I realized how much I'd missed our banter. It was our way of showing affection, and I felt there was an enormous chasm in my life.

"You're on, Daddy, although I'm really rusty."

"It's been a long time, Amy."

"Sure has. Almost as though I'd been away."

I had followed him into the den where he proceeded to take the Scrabble set off the bookshelf while I unfolded a stacking table.

"You have been away," he said, as we sat down opposite each other, "on a long journey. But you're here now."

I had to swallow hard to keep from crying. "Wasn't much of a trip," I said. "I mean. . . ."

"I know what you mean," he said, and smiled at me so fondly that I didn't have to say another word. From the look in his eyes, I could tell that he knew he had his daughter back.

The gym had been transformed into a glittering ballroom. Twinkling lights were strung everywhere, shimmering paper lined the walls, silver balloons drifted along the ceiling, and luminescent paper cloths were draped over the refreshment tables. The band was playing a slow piece when Jeff and I arrived. It was almost as though it had been planned that way, and we both wanted to take advantage of it.

"Here's our chance, Jeff, before they change the pace."

"I'm with you, Amy," Jeff said, sliding one crutch under the bleacher where we were standing.

Then he grasped me with his free arm and

together we swayed to the music. We hardly moved our feet, but for me it was more romantic than any dance had ever been.

"Amy," Jeff whispered, "I really can lean on you, can't I?"

"You know it," I breathed, and if possible, I held him even closer.

WILDFIRE®

Move from one breathtaking love story to another with the Hottest Teen Romances in town!

NEW WILDFIRES! $2.25 each

☐ UH33328-3   **LOVING THAT O'CONNOR BOY** Diane Hoh

☐ UH33180-9   **SENIOR DREAMS CAN COME TRUE**
Jane Claypool Miner

☐ UH33268-6   **LOVE SIGNS** M.L. Kennedy

☐ UH33266-X   **MY SUMMER LOVE** Elisabeth Ogilvie

BEST-SELLING WILDFIRES!

☐ UH32890-5   **THE BOY NEXT DOOR** Vicky Martin $2.25

☐ UH33265-1   **OUT OF BOUNDS** Eileen Hehl $2.25

☐ UH33097-7   **CHRISTY'S SENIOR YEAR** Maud Johnson $2.25

☒ UH32284-2   **ANGEL** Helen Cavanagh $2.25

☐ UH32542-6   **MISS PERFECT** Jill Ross Klevin $1.95

☐ UH32431-4   **LOVE GAMES** Deborah Aydt $1.95

☐ UH32536-1   **KISS AND TELL** Helen Cavanagh $2.25

☐ UH31931-0   **SENIOR CLASS** Jane Claypool Miner $1.95

☐ UH33096-9   **CHRISTY'S LOVE** Maud Johnson $2.25

☐ UH32846-8   **NICE GIRLS DON'T** Caroline B. Cooney $2.25

Scholastic Inc.,
P.O. Box 7502, 2932 E. McCarty St., Jefferson City, MO 65102

Please send me the books I have checked above. I am enclosing
$_____ (please add $1.00 to cover shipping and handling).
Send check or money order–no cash or C.O.D.'s please.

Name _____

Address _____

City_____ State/Zip _____

Please allow four to six weeks for delivery.   WDF 852

Join the Team!

They're talented. They're fabulous-looking. They're winners! And they've got what you want! Don't miss any of these exciting CHEERLEADERS books!

Watch for these titles! $2.25 each

Books chosen with you in mind from

point

—Pass the word.

**ving...loving...growing.
hat's what POINT books are all about!
hey're books you'll love reading and
ill want to tell your friends about.**

on't miss these other exciting Point titles!

EW POINT TITLES! $2.25 each

]QI 33306-2	**The Karate Kid** B.B. Hiller	
]QI 31987-6	**When We First Met** Norma Fox Mazer	
]QI 32512-4	**Just the Two of Us** Hila Colman	
]QI 32338-5	**If This Is Love, I'll Take Spaghetti** Ellen Conford	
]QI 32728-3	**Hello...Wrong Number** Marilyn Sachs	
]QI 33216-3	**Love Always, Blue** Mary Pope Osborne	
]QI 33116-7	**The Ghosts of Departure Point** Eve Bunting	
]QI 33195-7	**How Do You Lose Those Ninth Grade Blues?** Barthe DeClements	
]QI 33550-2	**Charles in Charge** Elizabeth Faucher	
]QI 32306-7	**Take It Easy** Steven Kroll	
]QI 33409-3	**Slumber Party** Christopher Pike